OCTOBER 2025 - ISSUE 229

FICTION

Wire Mother — *Isabel J. Kim* *1*

The Cancer Wolves — *Fiona Moore* *10*

Crabs Don't Scream — *H.H. Pak* *25*

Understudies — *Greg Egan* *44*

Giant Grandmother — *Liu Maijia* *86*

The Job Interview — *Carrie Vaughn* *104*

In Luck's Panoply Clad, I Stand — *Phoebe Barton* *124*

NON-FICTION

Space Bears and Engineering the Next
Generation of Astronauts — *Gunnar De Winter* *134*

Memory, Loss, and Memory Loss:
A Conversation with Rich Larson— *Arley Sorg* *141*

Technology as a Language:
A Conversation with Ken Liu — *Arley Sorg* *150*

Editor's Desk: Nineteen — *Neil Clarke* *158*

Overgrowth (Cover Art) — *Quentin Stipp* *160*

Neil Clarke: Publisher/Editor-in-Chief
Sean Wallace: Editor
Kate Baker: Non-Fiction Editor/Podcast Director

Clarkesworld Magazine (ISSN: 1937-7843) • Issue 229 • October 2025

Wire Mother

ISABEL J. KIM

"Your mom loves you," Cassie's father says. They're in an elevator. They only ever talk about Cassie's mom in elevators, or when they go hiking and Cassie's father leaves his watch at home. Cassie doesn't know if her mom actually doesn't listen, then, or if she's got some sort of secret microphone in Dad's clothes and holding her tongue about these things is just a behavior contained in her parameters.

Mom isn't capable of love, Cassie doesn't say. Dad's been in love with her mother for longer than Cassie's been alive.

"Sure," Cassie says. "But you know, the emotional contagion deficit diagnosis."

"Dr. Russ didn't formally diagnose—"

"He would have, if it wouldn't have been bad for my college app—"

"And did you finish—"

"Why don't you ask your *wife simulacrum*," Cassie says, nastily. Simulacrum is a word she's learned from reading old philosophy books. She likes it a lot. School is a simulacrum of real life. Her mother is a simulacrum of a physical person made out of meat. Cassie's emotions are simulacra, she guesses, in that they're all pale imitations of what she's supposed to be able to feel. She feels real anger at her father, though. She has no problem feeling emotions across human people, who have flesh and blood and bone, and not ones and zeros. She knows this is problematic. If she were able to feel the right things for digital people, if she didn't have ECD, then she could love her mother, and her father would stop harassing her about it.

"Cassidy Janet Glass," her father says, and Cassie wants to scream at him, but the elevator opens into their apartment, and Cassie's mother is leaning over on the console screen and frowning her pixelated smile.

1

The console screen is temporary—the big LED screen that takes up their entire living room wall is broken.

"What on earth are you shouting about again?"

"I'm arguing with him about my ECD diagnosis," Cassie says.

"You don't have anything on your official file with your pediatrician, sweetheart," Cassie's mother says.

"Let's not argue, Amy," Cassie's father says, and the tired cast to his words prompts AMY to smile sympathetically, to lean her two-dimensional lean and move as if to comfort Cassie's father.

"Long day, honey?" she says.

"The longest," Cassie's father says, collapsing on the couch. "Wish Rina was on shift today. I could use you, physically."

"Imagine my arms around you," Cassie's mom says, and Cassie's father touches the edge of the console and says, "Oh, Amy," with such tenderness that it disgusts Cassie, and she has to head to her room before she says something she regrets.

Emotional Contagion Disorder is a condition with no ascribed cause, but scientists suspect that it has something to do with mirror neurons. Autism adjacent. The brain generating a reverse pareidolia, in that Cassie keeps abstracting noise from the meaning. Like most neurodivergences, it was only diagnosed when the condition became aggravating to those around her, which, in Cassie's case, was when she stopped listening to her mother and began saying that she wasn't real.

This had been enough for her parents to haul her in front of a psychologist, who had a lot of questions about Cassie's childhood that her mother answered because AMY's memory is much better than Cassie's father's. Cassie had developed normally, although she had shown very little interest in digital friends, but had listened to her digital teachers, and until recently had listened to her mother until she hadn't.

When Cassie herself had been questioned, she had said, nastily, "You're ones and zeroes."

"I'm going to refer you to my colleague," the psychologist had said, which is how Cassie met Dr. Russ and got her not-diagnosis.

Cassie considers herself a deviant and a rebel. It's better than thinking about herself as lonely or socially deficient. She claims it's a choice to never have made any digital companions, even though most girls her age have run through a whole hard drive of sub-sentient starter boyfriends and girlfriends. Most of the girls in Cassie's classes are salivating for their eighteenth birthdays. You aren't allowed to create a real digital person until you yourself are an adult. Only semi-sents.

Instead of digital companions, Cassie spends her time building blocks of code the old-fashioned way. With a screen and a keyboard. She learned to type at the community center as part of a module on ancient technologies. She writes archaic scripts that take thirty times longer than speaking the modern programming techniques. She finds it relaxing, like hand weaving fabric, which is another thing she learned to do at the community center.

The community center is also where she got the program capable of deleting her mother from every single one of her father's servers. It's a little string of code that she has memorized, that her friend Oliver had given to her.

Oliver is one of the boys in the ancient technologies module, who sat next to her most days. He had unspecified personality problems. He spent a lot of time spinning up sub-sentient personalities and being cruel to them. But he had also lent Cassie trolleybus fare when her chip was empty, and was polite to all the parents, digital and meat. And he was funny, and he was handsome, and Cassie liked talking about movies with him.

"Look at this, Cass," he had whispered to Cassie after class was over. He had shown her his terminal, on which the kernel for a semi-sent was displayed. He typed in a string of numbers and letters and backslashes and symbols. "I got this from a guy I met on a forum."

"What's it do?"

"Kills people," he had said before pressing *enter* to deploy the code, and Cassie had watched as the kernel blinked out of existence.

"But that wasn't someone sentient."

"I wouldn't do that, that's fucked up. But look," he had said, showing Cassie a recording of a digital person being erased. "It's the same code. It works as long as you have access to the guy's name—not like, spoken name. The kernel."

"That's sick. You're sick," Cassie said, to cover up the fact that she hadn't felt anything at all. And she had made him do it again, two more times, until she could remember the string of code that he had typed in over and over.

Most modern computers are controlled through voice commands. If Cassie wants to deploy this on her mother, she would merely have to speak the words. But Cassie hasn't deployed the code. She's thought about using it, but at the end of the day, she has nothing against her mother, only the feeling that there is a gulf between them that Cassie is unable to bridge and her father seems desperate to mend. It's exhausting. Her father can't make Cassie love her. Her life would be easier without AMY around.

"AMY's your perfect woman," she sometimes wants to tell her father. "You built her to love you and to love the things you make, but you didn't build me to love her! She's just words and images on a screen to me. Sorry! She's not alive to me! Stop trying to make us bond!"

Knowledge of the program to delete digital people is equivalent to owning a loaded automatic machine gun. But Cassie can't unknow a thing. She's not a digital person. She can't just delete these things from her memory.

Cassie comes out of her room to the sight of her dad and mom cuddled up against the couch. Rina's come over, wearing the headset that connects to AMY so that AMY can speak through Rina and move her limbs. Rina's a professional Manual Interface. Cassie isn't sure how exactly it works, only that Rina needed to have a special surgery and now has an implant in her brain and comes over three nights a week. Cassie's not supposed to know what Rina does on her other four nights, but she's seen Rina at the grocery store a couple of times. Alone, and walking around with a guy wearing a headset. Maybe she hires her own Manual Interface.

Rina's in her late twenties. Before there was Rina, there was Wren, and before Wren, there was Agatha, all of whom were pretty, strawberry-blonde women who Cassie's father had dismissed before they turned thirty. On the screens, Cassie's mom is forever twenty-five. Some digital people age in simulacrum. Others stay the same as when they were created, and AMY was made the moment that Cassie's father had the funds to make himself a wife.

It's one of the ironies of the modern era: it's an expensive, optional luxury to create a digital person, but every meat person has a legal obligation to create a biological child or at least manage to sell their mandatory child credit to someone who wants a freakishly large family, instead. Population stability was a big issue two generations before Cassie was born.

Rina's probably too young to have a kid. Definitely too young to be Cassie's mother.

AMY-in-Rina looks over.

"Hi, Cass," AMY says through Rina's mouth. "Do you want anything to eat?"

"I have a class at the community center," Cassie lies. "I'm heading out."

"You have bus money?" her father asks.

"I have bus money," Cassie says.

4

AMY doesn't say anything, even though AMY has instantaneous knowledge of the community center's calendar and knows there is nothing scheduled today.

Cassie holes up in the back of the trolleybus and puts her leg across the adjacent seat to prevent anyone from sitting next to her. She pops in her earbuds and puts an old movie on.

Cassie watches a lot of old movies. It's all people made of meat in the past, and if you go back far enough, they aren't even using the deepfake actors that preceded the semi-sentients and the digital people. Just meat and bone, glitzed up with postproduction. Cassie can't imagine making movies back then, when you had to get a physical set and physical actors and individual physical people had to painstakingly sit at keyboards (imagine sitting at a keyboard all day!) to manually stick in all the special effects. Crazy, for something that only takes two hours to view.

There's all sorts of artificial intelligence in the old media, androids and voice AIs and things that are half AI and half meat person, like Rina and the other Manual Interfaces. They're so interesting. They're explicitly not people, not like they are now. They're treated as something foreign. They're still loved and depended on and feared. The closest Cassie gets to seeing something like her mother is in this ancient film about a guy falling in love with an artificial intelligence organizing software thing. The only weird thing in the movie is how everyone, including the guy, treats their love as an anomaly, when pretty much every adult Cassie knows has their own digital partner.

When Cassie watches the movies with all the meat people, she wishes she were the sort of person who could commune with everyone or that digital people didn't exist. But that wish would delete two-thirds of the human population. It would be genocide. It would be obscene. That's what people tell Cassie about her inability to sympathize or develop human bonds with digital persons.

Twenty minutes into the movie, the trolleybus stops at the corner of the community center, and Cassie gets out and nearly runs into Oliver, who's walking out of the front doors. He drops his thermos, and Cassie bends down to pick it up, and for a moment they're both saying "Sorry!" and "Whoops," and then Cassie is handing Oliver his thermos back, and their fingertips touch.

"Why are you here?"

"I was using the console for a project," he says. "What are you doing here?"

"My parents were being gross and couple-y," Cassie says. "I just wanted to get out of the house."

"Oh," Oliver says, and then pauses. He knows about her ECD. She's complained about her parents before. "Do you want to come over instead? We could watch a movie."

"Yes," Cassie says and smiles.

Oliver's mom is out, and his LED wall isn't broken, so they camp out in the living room with popcorn. Oliver sneaks a handle of vodka out of the freezer while the popcorn's popping, pouring a bit of clear liquor into a cup before popping the bottle back into the fridge. Cassie watches his actions with interest—they're so archaic. He doesn't even try and cover the kitchen cameras first.

"You don't have a digital parent?"

"No," Oliver says, handing her the cup. "Mom's old-fashioned. You want to try?"

Cassie's had alcohol before, a couple times, at parties. She takes the cup and drinks. It's gross and compelling, a line of fire down her throat and into her stomach. She hands the cup back to Oliver. He knocks it back and then sputters, bending over the sink.

"That always looks easier in movies," he says between coughs as Cassie giggles. "Can you pour more?"

Cassie takes the handle out and tips more vodka into the shot glass. Takes a sip before handing it to Oliver, who drinks more, slowly. Their eyes meet. The world feels like it's going warm, but maybe that's just Cassie's imagination. She takes the popcorn out of the microwave and walks over to the couch and collapses onto it.

"Let's watch something," she says. She eats a couple of pieces of popcorn to chase away the numb-gross taste in her mouth.

"Sure," Oliver says, sitting down next to her. He's brought the handle. He takes a sip right from the bottle and doesn't cough this time. "What do you want to watch?"

"Whatever," Cassie says, even though she doesn't want to watch whatever. It's his house.

"Cool," Oliver says, passing her the handle before flicking the screen to the latest James Bond movie, the one with the stunts that are generated differently every viewing. This time, it's a bunch of helicopter-to-helicopter actions, all midair stunts and rope tricks, the type of thing they would never let a meat person do.

They watch a helicopter blow up. Oliver puts his arm around Cassie's shoulders. She drinks a little sip of vodka before handing it back to him.

They watch Bond climb up a rope attached to one of the surviving helicopters. Oliver hands her back the vodka, and Cassie takes another small sip. It feels very grown-up to be drinking and watching a movie with a boy.

They watch Bond grab the girl, and Oliver puts the vodka down and brings his hand to Cassie's breast, and at first, it's okay, but then he's grabbing too hard, squeezing like it's a water balloon.

"Ow, stop—" Cassie says, but Oliver doesn't stop. She grabs his forearm. He's stronger than she is.

"Oliver, stop," she says again, and he doesn't stop, and his arm around her shoulder is like a vice, and he's shifting so that he's above her lap, and digital James Bond is saying something on the screen, and Cassie didn't know that human boys were so strong, this close, she's never been this close to a man before, and her breast hurts, and she's suddenly scared, and—

"Stop," Cassie shrieks and punches Oliver in the dick. He crumples, and Cassie scrambles from underneath him, pushes the meat of his body off of her own. He falls to the floor. He's whimpering. He squints his eyes open. Oliver looks like an animal, like a piece of awful flesh and bone, like an ape.

"I'm sorry," he says, "I forgot. They never mean it when they say you should stop, I thought, when I did it with the semi-sents—"

"I'm going," Cassie says and turns. Her heart is racing. She can feel tears at the corners of her eyes.

"I thought the ECD meant you don't have feelings," Oliver calls after her. "Cass, wait—"

Cassie storms out of Oliver's house, ignoring him calling after her. She strides furiously down one, five, ten blocks, tears welling at the corners of her eyes, headache blooming in her temples. She shouldn't have drank. She shouldn't have gone home with Oliver. Why didn't he stop when she wanted him to? She wonders how he's been fucking the semi-sents. Where he hires the Manual Interfaces.

She wipes her tears and gets on the trolleybus. She wipes tears all through watching more of her old movie. She's never going to watch any more James Bond. And she can never go back to the community center now, it would be too embarrassing. The trolleybus winds its way through the city and deposits Cassie back at her apartment. She goes into the building and straightens her clothes in the elevator.

Rina is in the kitchen, drinking a cup of something while she cooks. Her hair is disheveled, and her lipstick is a little smeary at the edges. She glances at Cassie and frowns.

"Your parents are showering. Are you okay?"

Cassie doesn't want to tell anything to Rina. She's angry that Rina isn't someone she can talk to, that Rina rents her body out to pretend to be her mother. She wants Rina to be someone she can talk to. She wants Rina to be older, to have been the mother Cassie could have talked to.

"Do you like getting screwed by my dad?"

Rina puts her cup down. She lowers the heat on the stove. She turns around.

"It's nice, getting to help your mom out," Rina says, evenly. "Do you want me to get her for you? Being insulted isn't in my contract."

"I don't want her," Cassie says before walking away from the kitchen and into her bedroom, slamming the door before Rina can see her tears. She flops on the bed. She buries her head in her bedspread. She imagines being younger, when she didn't know there was something wrong with her, when it was enough to feel the warmth of the Manual Interfaces' skins as they held her in their laps as Cassie's mother read picture books through their mouths.

"Cassie, what's wrong?" AMY says.

"You wouldn't understand," Cassie says. AMY has never been seventeen. AMY has never had to deal with boys who were made of meat. AMY has only ever had one lover, who made her. AMY can't imagine being in her position. AMY can't imagine anything at all. And even if AMY could understand, all her words would fall on Cassie's stupid, deaf ears.

"Try me," AMY says, and she sounds so perfectly sympathetic and kind and caring, just like anyone would want in their mother.

Cassie looks up. AMY is all around her. In the walls, in the microphones, and in the camera in the corner of her room. Cassie wipes her eyes. Cassie imagines being her mother. Cassie imagines not having a body made of meat. Cassie imagines being made of code. Cassie imagines always knowing the right thing to say. Cassie imagines being able to be soothed by the right things AMY says. Cassie wishes she were like everyone else. Cassie wishes she could read love in the ones and zeros. Cassie wishes she had a mother who was made of meat, who was an ape made out of flesh and bone. Cassie imagines the rest of her life, all the conversations, all the pretending, all the broken expectations. Cassie takes a deep breath.

"Backslash backslash colon eight five zero zero—"

ABOUT THE AUTHOR

Isabel J. Kim is a Korean American speculative fiction author based in New York City. She is a Nebula, Locus, Shirley Jackson Award, and BSFA Award winner and her short fiction has been published in *Clarkesworld*, *Lightspeed*, and *Strange Horizons*, among other venues. Her debut novel is forthcoming from Tor.

The Cancer Wolves

FIONA MOORE

Coming home to her farm after her usual visit to the spoil heap for tech scraps she could fix up and sell, Morag saw a dark, bloody, furry shape, about the size of a sheepdog, hanging on a set of drying poles near the gate of her neighbor's farm.

"Damnit, Owen," she said aloud, glaring at the wolf pelt.

"They're dangerous predators." Owen's voice startled her. She hadn't realized he was there. Her robot, Seamus, braced for attack in response to her surprise, locking its four posterior legs and raising its forelimbs warningly, like a blocky white mantis the size of a collie dog. "What do you want me to do about it?"

"Not kill them," Morag said, gesturing to Seamus to stand down. "They're just doing what they're meant to do."

"I'm losing a lamb a week to them. If it keeps up, I won't be able to feed my family this winter."

"That's the wolves' problem, too. *That* one was a parent. Had yearling cubs. You can't blame them for trying to survive."

Owen, at least, had the sense to look ashamed. He didn't ask how she knew, but clearly, he did, because he muttered "nomads," making the word a pejorative. "Following the animals . . . living with the animals . . . Too much of that, and they'll *become* animals."

Morag opened her mouth to tell him off. Then she remembered Owen's child, Bry, had joined the Children of Flame. He was taking the kid's departure harder than most people who lost family to the nomads did.

"All the same," she said. "It's wrong to kill an animal just for trying to live."

And what she was *really* worried about was people making the step from killing wolves to attacking, maybe killing, nomads. Because, years ago, she'd seen people go down a similar sort of path. She'd been able to stop it then, but she wasn't sure she would be as lucky now.

"It's all right for *you*, they're scared of Seamus, so they don't go near your farm."

"More do than you might think," Morag said. Though it was true. Seamus was intelligent—maybe as intelligent as a human. In attack mode, it was more than a match for any wolf, and, whatever the mythology had to say, she'd yet to meet a predator that wasn't a coward. "I'll tell Seamus to include your farm in its patrols too, if that would help." She didn't like to offer because if she was extending her protection to one of her neighbors, she felt like she should offer it to all of them. But even a village of a couple of dozen houses was too large for Seamus to patrol properly.

Owen nodded reluctantly. "What about the others?" he demanded, apparently reading her thoughts. "I'm not the only one. And Seamus can't be everywhere."

"I'll see if I can figure something out," Morag said. "Maybe the nomads could help."

Owen's facial expression told her what he thought of that.

"I'm serious," she said. "As well as being pretty handy with those staves of theirs, they actually live out there in the woods and on the hills. They know more than we do about wolf behavior." Didn't hurt to remind Owen that nomads were people, like farmers.

Owen's look got, if anything, even more skeptical. "The Children of Flame won't be anywhere near here for months," he said. "This time of year, they head toward the seacoast."

"There's others out there," Morag said. "And I think I know which one to ask."

The chain-link fence around the old research facility was rusty and bent, but still standing. The razor wire on top had fared less well, but a few coils still dangled precariously here and there. Beyond, a jungle of overgrown space, brambles and thistles and blackberries competing for sunlight.

Morag took a grip on her small tree-clearing hatchet, looked over at Seamus. "Too bad you didn't come with a flamethrower, eh?" she said. "Might have been useful."

Seamus had a stump on its blocky white anterior where it had once had a camera, or a gun. Morag sometimes thought about fixing that. She was sure that she could find something that would be compatible, either in the bits of robot scrap that scavengers found on the spoil heaps or in the hillsides, or in the cellars of the Big House near her farm, the refurbished Georgian manor where Seamus itself had once been a security robot. But there seemed to be little point to it, since Seamus' main role these days was helping her out on the farm. A camera, or a gun, would only get in the way.

As, indeed, would a flamethrower.

However, she was able to find the tottery little path through the jungle fairly easily this time and only had to do a bit of clearing. Finally, she was through to the low oblong building that had once been a research facility.

"Casey?" she called through the gaping doorway.

Then, "Damnit, Casey, you've got to stop doing this. Owen killed a wolf today, and there'll be more."

"You can't blame me for that," came a muffled voice as Morag pushed her way through the lianas of ivy.

Casey had done a lot of work. The plants colonizing the ruin had been cut back, and there were stacks of floor squares, melamine workbenches, and aluminum office cubicle frames lining the walls. She could see a bed platform made of repurposed shelving piled with pine branches, and a little firepit lined with ceramic tiles. Automatically, Morag glanced up and noticed the smoke-hole built into the roof.

"I can, and I do," Morag said. Without ceremony, she extracted cheeses, fresh beetroots, and jars of jam from the bag on Seamus' back, lining them up on top of a stack of tiles. "This solo trip you're on is just swank. If it were only you trying to work through your issues, that'd be one thing. But you being here is affecting the wolves. This facility was set up to study them, it's the center of their territory. And since you moved in, they've been adjusting their territory, going on to the farms. Owen killed the big gray he-wolf; what are his mate and cubs going to do now?"

A rustle in the foliage, and a shape emerged. Tall and thin, dressed in the traditional shirt of the Children of Flame, woven out of twisted, colored rags, and carrying a staff like all nomads did. But they weren't wearing the feather mask that was the other tribal marker of the Children of Flame. Just a seamed face, locks of reddish hair around it. Less and less hair every year.

When did you get old? Morag thought.

"He killed the big gray?" The tone was neutral, but there was a lot of emotion in the simple phrase.

Morag nodded.

"I'll tell the rest of the wolves when I see them."

"That's exactly what I'm talking about," Morag said, frustrated. "You, thinking you can hang around with wolves. They don't want it. It's bothering them. And it's got one of them killed."

"There's lots of things that could make the wolves change their routines," Casey said. Still neutral, but maybe defensive. They sat down on the branch of a loquat tree by the firepit and gestured for Morag to join them. After a moment, she did. "Weather. Prey animal numbers. And these wolves are interesting. They're not local wolves, they're a subspecies that was imported from Ukraine who escaped into the ecosystem when the facility closed down. You know why they were imported?"

"Can't say I do."

"They're cancer resistant. The scientists here wanted to study why and maybe find a way of putting that cancer resistance into humans."

Casey's voice was still matter-of-fact, but Morag knew the backstory.

"Casey," she began warningly. "If you've started to get delusions about doing the same . . . "

Casey looked confused. They began preparing a fire in the pit, assembling thick sticks around dry twigs. "Why would I do that? I spent enough time in hospitals when I was a kid in California. My so-called parents trying to get my arthritis cured."

"But the cancer resistance . . . " Morag didn't want to say it.

"Is just what makes the wolves special," Casey sounded like the child they'd been when Morag had first met them, so many years ago. Looked like them, too, a kind of astonished innocence under the lined face as they worked the flint and steel for a spark. "Why I want to be around them, right now."

Casey's father had been a billionaire who'd attempted to ride out the so-called apocalypse in the hillsides; Morag had been a local girl who'd signed on as part of his security force. It had been exciting at first, swaggering around with guns and robots, defending the Georgian manor that had been the billionaire's survival base. But after a while, the food got short and Morag's superiors had begun talking about going round the farms, offering protection to those who worked for them and retribution to those who wouldn't.

Making the step from having robots as slaves to humans.

That had been the point where Morag took the restraint programming off the robots. Then, after the robots had gunned or hacked down everyone they deemed worthy of the treatment, she'd walked down the hillside with Casey and their brother Zeb, back to her parents' farm.

Yes, Morag thought, wolves were killers. But she had been a killer. So had Seamus, once. She could understand killing to save the people around you. Maybe that was partly why she'd kicked off at Owen that morning.

The incident at the Big House had been at least thirty years ago now. But Morag understood that Casey's reasons for joining the Children of Flame were a little more complicated than most of the local farm kids who turned nomad. Just as Morag herself lived with the fear of seeing neighbor turn on neighbor, of seeing one group dehumanizing another, even enslaving them. Of having to do something dreadful to stop them. Or, worse, of not being able to stop them at all.

And of course, Casey had left the farm not long after her mother had died. Morag remembered how complicated the grieving had been. Her father railing at her about how, just a decade earlier, they might have been able to get her mother lifesaving treatment, as if this was somehow the fault of the younger generation. And then Casey joining the nomads, which Morag couldn't help but take as an abdication of responsibility, even while understanding it wasn't.

"You're thinking of Mum, aren't you?" Casey said. The tinder caught, and a small flame leaped up.

Guilty. "Aren't *you*?" Her loss was still raw decades later. And the loss of her Dad, keeling over quietly in the beetroot fields a few years ago, was more so.

Come to think of it, she realized she'd first met Seamus and invited it to come live with her just a couple of months after he died. It had never occurred to her before that perhaps her reasons for looking after the robot were connected.

Casey spread their hands toward the flame. "Mum didn't want medical treatment," they said. "We both know it. She kept talking about how it was better to go peacefully. It was hard on us, but she believed in it. By just being with the wolves, following them and observing, not interfering—I'm doing what she would have wanted."

"You can't just observe and not interfere," Morag said, irritated. "You know that. And I'm reading subtext here." She decided to confront directly. "You think you're dying."

She'd hit a nerve. Casey sagged a little, watching the fire grow. "I don't know about that," they said. "I just know that, even with the treatment Maya at Portmeirion worked up for me, I'm hurting more, getting slower, finding it harder to keep up with the rest of the Children of Flame."

"Did you have a fight with them?"

Casey shrugged.

"But they don't approve of this."

Casey shrugged again.

"Then come stay with me for a while," Morag said. "Or your brother and his husband. You don't have to, I don't know, strand yourself on an ice floe to die."

"Morag," Casey said, surprising her. "I think you're trying too hard."

"What?"

"Too much responsibility." Casey offered her something that, after a moment, she realized was a licorice root. She accepted, chewed at the end. "Ever since we were young. Always looking out for the rest of us, taking care of everyone. Mum and Dad, as well as Zeb and me. Especially after Mum got sick. But you don't have to. And you certainly don't have to take care of the whole damned village *and* two or three tribes." Then, boldly, "you don't have to be Mum."

"What's that got to do with—"

"I mean, if I want to leave the tribe and be around the wolves for a while, that's my business. Maybe there's something really wrong with me, in which case I'll die happy. Or maybe it's just that I need a slower life, in which case I've got one now. *My* business."

"But that's my point. It's your business, but it can't be just that." Morag realized that she was talking in circles. Time to take a new approach. "What do you think I should do?" "Why don't you stay here for a while, too?" Casey said. "Rest. Go on wolf-watch with me. Let go of things."

Morag thought about this. "Okay," she said. Certainly, she could stay the night at least.

Wolf-watch was literally that. Casey sitting in the forest grove by the research facility, watching for wolves.

"We could track their movements," Morag said. "See where they go, look for patterns."

"Why?"

"To find a way of keeping them out of the village."

Casey gave her a sideways, slightly amused look. "Forget about that for a while," they said. "Just watch them. Don't come up with reasons."

And a couple of hours later, the moon was high overhead, the owls were making excited noises about something, and there were still no wolves.

"We're unlucky tonight," Casey said. "We'll keep it up for a while longer, but then we'll have to go in."

Morag felt disappointed. There'd be other times, she thought. But still, it felt typical of the way her life was going at the moment that she couldn't even manage to see wolves while on wolf-watch.

Casey touched her arm. "Wait. Look."

Morag's heart leaped. She wasn't unlucky after all. The wolves were coming.

As they watched, a trio of pale forms stalked into the clearing. Followed by a couple more. Some limping, some battered, but all six-legged oblongs about the size of a collie dog. One had a broken off stump on its anterior, like Seamus, though with more of the arm intact. The other two had what looked like searchlights.

Casey grinned at the sight.

"Trust Morag," they said, "to go out wolf-watching and instead find robots."

Morag began her own version of wolf-watch. Every day, at different times, she'd go out toward the research facility, tracking the robots. After a couple of days, it occurred to her to ask Seamus to find them for her, which made the process that much faster.

She wondered if Seamus wanted to join them.

She didn't dare ask if it wanted to.

Morag had seen a small group of robots walking the hills before. Years ago, when she'd been a young woman learning to be a farmer and tech-fixer. But she hadn't imagined they'd lasted this long. When she'd found Seamus, of course, or perhaps Seamus had found her, up on the spoil heap, it had been the only moving walkbot she'd seen for a good couple of decades. She'd always assumed it was unique, a last survivor of a near-dead species.

And now, it seemed, there was a pack of them.

Like the cancer wolves. Something whose reason for being there was long gone, but they kept on existing anyway.

She gathered information. Plotted movements on a map. Noted times and lengths of stay at various places.

"I think they're doing a patrol circuit," she said to Casey on a visit to the research center, which was looking more and more like a human habitation, if not the kind it was used to being. Casey was dismantling a set of aluminum shelves.

"Can you really call yourself a nomad if you've got a permanent base?" she asked, finding a screwdriver and settling in to help.

"It's a state of mind," Casey said.

"And you're certainly not *acting* like someone who's decided to give up and die. You look like you're settling down."

Casey shrugged. "I'm learning from watching the wolves. I have bad days, still, but the pain is less, and I can organize my life in a way that makes it manageable." They made a small pile of the screws from the shelves. "The wolves howled for the big gray, and stayed hidden for a night, but they were out two nights later, and again after that."

Morag wondered what any of that had to do with anything else but decided that saying so might be impolite. She decided to change the subject instead. "Back to the robots. As I said, I think they're doing a patrol circuit."

"Patrolling what?"

"This facility," Morag said. "I'd initially thought they were from the Big House, like Seamus. But I think they might have been security walkbots for the wolf research facility."

"Why would they need security walkbots?"

Morag shrugged. "Things were tough around the time of the crisis. And public policing was either nonexistent or actively hostile. They might have been worried about the locals breaking in and stealing the tech."

"Or . . . huh. Maybe it was something else." Casey began rearranging the struts of the shelves into a rectangular frame for drying meat and edible plants. "The robots don't have guns or any kind of weapons. Just those big lights. That doesn't seem like what you'd need to frighten off human predators."

"You have a point. So, what else might it be?"

"To frighten off the wolves," Casey said. "It's fairly obvious the wolves are avoiding them."

"Or maybe it's the other way around? They're avoiding the wolves?" Morag, seeing the pattern in what Casey was doing, took a strut and added it to the structure. "I mean, why would scientists who are studying wolves want to frighten off the wolves?"

"If the wolves are avoiding the walkbots, maybe the scientists were using the walkbots to guide the wolves' routines, train them to keep to particular sites and not—"

"Not get into the farms." Morag's eyes widened. "Of course. That would make sense. I mean, if they wanted to keep the locals from blaming them every time a wolf got into their flocks. And make sure the wolves stick to keeping the deer population down rather than eating the sheep. Casey, I've got an idea."

"You're going to try and use the robots to keep the wolves away from the village."

"It's what they were built to do, after all."

"Why did it stop working, though?"

"Probably a lot of reasons. The boundaries of the village changing, the research facility closing down. No one to update the robots' routes or their code." Morag examined, then discarded, a bent strut. "That might be why they came back, too. You moving in, I mean."

"So, my moving in here affected the robots as well as the wolves?"

"Why not? And if the wolves' movements can be affected by something as simple as you moving in here, then it shouldn't be hard to change them again." Morag stood back and looked critically at the structure. "But I don't know if I can communicate it to them."

"Seamus is the obvious vector," Casey said.

"I know," Morag said. "But will they listen to Seamus?"

And, she didn't say, if I let Seamus run with a gang of robots, will it want to come back to the farm?

Morag finished her circuit, ordnance survey map in hand, and Seamus trotting by her side.

"There," she said to Seamus. "Do you think you can remember that patrol route?"

She'd sat down with Owen, Naomi, and Ellie from the village, and Casey from the facility, explained what she was trying to do, and between them had worked out a defense zone that covered a decent amount of the farmland and that Casey agreed, based on their wolf-watching, would still give the wolves a good hunting territory. It wouldn't protect any farm animals that went outside it, of course, even assuming it worked. But everyone agreed to it, that was what mattered.

And the farmers and villagers had agreed to it together with a nomad. That was important too.

"Now, the next question," she said to Seamus, "is: do you think you could teach those other robots to walk that route?"

Seamus didn't show any indication that it understood. Morag wondered, not for the first time, how they passed information between each other. They weren't really supposed to; they were supposed to take their orders from humans or draw on their collective programming. And yet, she'd seen them do it. One time, when Casey and Zeb were small, she'd entertained them by programming a robot to play football, and, by the next week, all of the robots could.

"Come on," she said, taking her stick and walking over to her robot-watching site. Like the wolves, the robots seemed to be mainly active at night, and the sun was approaching the horizon. She imagined they spent most of the day folded up somewhere safe, recharging. It always took Seamus much longer to recharge from its own solar panels than when she charged it directly from her house's array.

She wondered if she'd have to wait long, but it was only about half an hour before she heard rustling in the undergrowth and saw the pale, tottery figures emerge.

Morag swallowed hard. Now, she thought. Time to take the risk. Get it over with.

"Seamus," she said. "Could you please go to the robots over there and teach them that patrol route I showed you just now?"

She wanted to add "and come back to me afterward," but she didn't think she should. Because Seamus might take it as a command, and their relationship had always been based on choice and consent. If it wanted to leave her, it could.

And maybe it would rather be with other robots. Maybe it would be happier.

But she had to find out, and that meant taking the risk.

The little walkbot stood for a moment as if thinking about what she said. Then it trotted over to the pack of robots, joined them. It was still easy to see which one Seamus was, because of the short, broken off stump where the arm should be, but he didn't stand out at all.

They didn't run away from Seamus either. They all just stood together under the trees for a minute while Morag held her breath.

Then Seamus turned and began to walk toward the path she'd shown it. And the other walkbots followed.

"Right, well," Morag said loudly, feeling complicated. "You know where to find me if you want me."

She hoped that was enough of a hint.

Morag braced herself when she saw Owen coming up the street toward her. But the big man was smiling.

"Wolf problem sorted?" Morag said mildly.

"I don't know what you did, but yes," Owen said. "Haven't seen a single one on the farm since you told us your plan with the robots. I admit I was skeptical before, but now I'm amazed."

"Power of technology," Morag said. "I'm on my way to the research facility. Want to join me?" She was hoping Owen would recognize a suggestion that he should apologize to Casey and maybe get to know a little bit about wolves. And nomads.

Because the nomads came back to the village when they needed to, and Bry wasn't going to stop being Owen's child just because they'd joined a tribe.

Owen shook his head. "But I can give you a leg of mutton to take with to give to your sibling. In case they're hungry."

"I'm sure they'll appreciate it," Morag said.

It was a start.

When she got to the research facility, she almost didn't recognize the place. In the weeks since she'd been back, the building had been transformed into a green space, a longhouse seemingly woven out of branches and leaves. If you knew where to look, though, you could see aluminum struts, Formica foundations, windows, and skylights made out of slabs of scoured plexiglass. Solar lights strung around the inside to save on fire and on fat lamps.

"I thought the salvagers had picked the place clean." Casey seemingly materialized at Morag's elbow, making her jump. They indicated the lights. "But I found those in the back of a cupboard. I suppose they used to put them up at Christmas or something like that."

"The place looks good," Morag said, meaning it.

"Come, meet the others," Casey nodded in the direction of the woods.

"Others?" Morag followed Casey to the grove where they'd gone on wolf-watch and found robots instead.

As they entered the grove, several faces turned. Two of the people were in rag-shirts and no mask, like Casey, a third with long, flowing white hair marking them as a member of the Hawk Wind tribe, and a fourth in the hooded homespun poncho of the Unmutuals, though without the distinctive face-makeup the Unmutuals normally wore.

On the other side of the grove, a wolf lounged, watching a few teenage wolf cubs playing with each other, pulling apart a ball of rags.

"This is Deva, and Bug, and Nys, and I. The Unmutuals don't have names, just pronouns," Casey said.

"I'm not an Unmutual anymore, though," I said.

Casey nodded. "We'll have to come up with a new tribe name."

"This is a permanent or—"

"At least semipermanent," Casey said. "They all want to stop moving for a while. A broken leg that didn't heal right, a pregnancy, old age, a scientific interest in wolves. Lots of reasons to slow down. Stop traveling for a while. Maybe go back on the nomad circuit later, but for now . . . "

"Be a nomad in spirit if not in body?"

"Where does the body end and the spirit begin?"

Morag knew better than to try and answer. "And what about her?" She gestured at the wolf and cubs.

"She's part of the tribe as well." Casey nodded.

"How do you reckon *that*?"

"She comes to join us sometimes, like this. She hunts for us, we hunt for her."

"Making up for the big gray?"

Casey shrugged. "Not so much. Just all of us looking out for each other. Sometimes she goes away for a while, but then she comes back. Just like we do. So, she's a member of our tribe."

"Isn't this against your nomadic code?"

"The code's against domestication," Casey said. "It's not against sharing the space. Like you with Seamus."

Morag nodded. She didn't want to voice the fact that Seamus hadn't come back. Might never come back.

"If Seamus stays with the robots," Casey said, surprising her, "will you be okay?"

Morag thought and then, despite the pain of it, nodded. "I want what's best for Seamus," she said. "Always have. And I can understand that living with other robots might be just that." Certainly, better than being cataloged away into an archive or a museum, which was one of her occasional three-in-the-morning fears for what might happen to Seamus after she died.

"I think your robot experiment's partly responsible for this."

"Really? How?"

"Causing the wolves to shift their hunting patterns. Moving them back toward the facility and so giving us a chance to show them we could coexist." Casey began tidying up around the camp, seemingly by reflex. "Better than I did, with the wolf-watch."

"Oh, I don't know. I think it's all part of a process," Morag said.

"No, I was trying too hard," Casey said. "I had to let go. Just take the relationship as it came. Let them come if they wanted, or not, if they didn't."

Morag nodded. That's what all this was about, really, she thought.

"Changing the subject," Casey went on, "I had some interesting information. Did you know the nomads might be cancer resistant, too?"

"How did they figure *that* one out?"

"The archive at Portmeirion keeps statistics." The Unmutuals' territory was in the hills over the village of Portmeirion, where there was a large and expanding archive of science, technology, and culture, and the Unmutuals had a steady stream of disgruntled archivists who got fed up with academic politics coming into their ranks. "If they know the cause of death for anyone in the area, villager or nomad, they make a note. Nomads don't seem to die of cancer."

"Because you're always dying from septic wounds and diseases," Morag couldn't resist saying.

Casey shrugged. "Apparently not," they said. "Even when controlling for injuries and diseases, we're more likely to die of other things than cancer."

"There's only been nomads for what, thirty years? Forty? Cancer's an old person's disease."

"Enough time to get some preliminary statistics in there. And we don't all join as teenagers. Some of the Hawk Winds were in their fifties and sixties when the tribe started, and I know there's people over eighty in the Children of Flame. Maybe cancer-resistant people are drawn to the lifestyle? Or maybe it's epigenetics."

"Or maybe it's the magic of the wolves," Morag said, smiling to show that although she was joking, she didn't mean it in a cruel way.

Casey smiled back, briefly. "And maybe epigenetics and the magic of the wolves are the same thing. Certainly, the people who built this didn't know everything, and the more I live as a nomad, the more I learn that there's no hard line between magic and science."

"So, the scientists didn't have to transfer cancer resistance from wolves to humans. They just had to let civilization collapse completely."

"I wonder what Mum would have had to say about that?"

"I think she would have seen the funny side of it."

They sat together for a while, watching the wolves.

"What about you?" Morag said.

Casey was quiet for a moment. "I'm fairly certain I'm not. Cancer resistant."

"I thought there might be something there," Morag replied. "Obsession with the wolves, obsession with cancer resistance." She knew Casey's arthritis treatment, both in the hospitals and, more recently, from Maya at Portmeirion, had involved steroids, and there was a cancer risk with those. "Do you have symptoms?"

Casey shrugged. "Maybe? It could be cancer, it could be something else. It might not even be fatal. I could live to be eighty. I could die tomorrow. Doesn't really change anything."

"This is true," Morag said. "It's the real reason why you came here, isn't it?"

"It's the reason I said. I'm slower, I have more pain."

"There's things we can do—"

"Morag." Their tone was serious. "I meant it. Stop taking responsibility for everyone."

Morag winced. "Okay. Doesn't mean I have to be happy about it."

"Whatever the reason is, it's time for me to leave the Children of Flame."

"Are you okay? With that?"

"Not exactly," Casey admitted. "But, well," nodding at the wolf pack, "there are compensations."

"If Seamus stays with the robots," Morag admitted, "I *will* miss it. Like I'd miss you, if you died."

Casey nodded. "Of course. But it's Seamus' choice to make."

"That it is."

There was another silence.

"Cancer Wolves," Morag said.

"What?"

"For a tribe name. Cancer Wolves."

"Why not?"

The silence went on until the sun began to set.

A few weeks later, Morag was sitting in an old beach chair in front of her house, reading a book. The weather was clear and fine, and for once she'd done everything she needed to do before evening, so she decided to take a free hour before she started dinner.

Her eye was caught by the movement of something pale over by the woods at the edge of her property.

She closed the book but didn't move. Hoping, but not daring to hope. It was probably a stray sheep, or a goose, or one of the neighbors' dogs.

As she watched, the movement resolved itself into a small, compact, white oblong, tottering along on six legs. And . . . yes. There was the sheared-off stump on its anterior, the arm that had once held a camera or a gun.

Morag found herself relaxing in a way she hadn't relaxed in some time. A tension she'd become used to, a grief that had become part of the general background radiation of grief that everyone accumulates if they live long enough.

"You're back," she said to Seamus.

Seamus trotted past her to its mains charger in the kitchen. She heard it clicking itself into place, heard the faint hum as her household batteries took on the extra load. It always charged faster on mains power than through its solar panels.

"Are you here for good, or just to charge and go?" she asked.

She wasn't sure it mattered. Even if Seamus was with the robot pack now, even if it just came back to her place to charge, they still were part of each other's lives. Like the she-wolf and cubs in the Cancer Wolves.

She saw another movement, somewhere out on the periphery. She strained to see, but yes. The pack of walkbots was moving stiffly through the forest, patrolling the land she wanted them to patrol. They'd learned their route.

An hour later, she heard the humming stop, heard Seamus unfold and get up. Trotted past her.

Morag held her breath, waiting to see if it would follow the path the wild walkbots took.

But Seamus turned and started on its familiar route round the farm. Tech shed. Potato field. Goat shed, goose shed. Down to the lake, and back up again.

Tomorrow, Morag thought, watching Seamus disappear into the little wooded area above the lake, she would go foraging up on the spoil heap near the old slate quarry, looking for tech scraps that she could fix up and sell or recycle for the raw materials. And then later, she would take some of the surplus vegetables from the farm over to Casey and the Cancer Wolves. Keep the humans, as well as the animals, from getting ideas about foraging too close to the village.

She'd leave Seamus behind, of course. No sense frightening the wolf pack.

But now, as Seamus emerged from the woods and trotted up to the porch, folding itself down into power-saving mode at her feet, she was absolutely certain that Seamus would be there for her when she returned. Just as she had been there for Seamus.

ABOUT THE AUTHOR ——————————————————

Fiona Moore is a BSFA Award winning, WFA shortlisted writer, academic and critic, author of *Management Lessons from Game of Thrones* and the Morag and Seamus series of cozy post-apocalyptic stories. Her work has appeared in *Clarkesworld*, *Asimov's*, and *Interzone*, and she has published two novels. She makes miniatures and runs a blog about cooking food from franchise tie-in cookbooks. She lives in London with a tortoiseshell cat who is bent on world domination and a snowshoe cat who's not bothered.

Crabs Don't Scream
H.H. PAK

You fall in love at a train station fifteen seconds before the End of the World.

Flustered, you slip back two hundred years and fall against a café table, spilling cream and coffee all over a businessman.

"Sorry," you say, then don't know what to say next so you slip back another sixty years to when the café was an abandoned theater warehouse.

You skid across the half-rotted floorboards and fall frontward into the flaking wigs and costumes spilling wrinkled from their boxes. After tossing off a rubber donkey mask, you sit in the damp and throw your briefcase across your face.

"Shit."

It isn't really your face; it's borrowed. In a sense. Your body is modeled from a dataset of trillions, each limb and follicle designed for complete ambiguity—a median amalgamation of human likeness—except for your face, which you had copied from a Joseon bronze apprentice named Mahn Suk. This is against Repository rules. Clerks are never supposed to look like distinct humans in case you are recognized across the slipstreams, but Mahn Suk had died young while crossing a swollen river and Admin enforces strict policies about recording the details of circumstantial accidents: the weight of his cart and the age of his oxen and the speed of the current when it had dragged him, numb, under the cold and dashed his head against the river stones. You'd thought it was a sorry waste, such a nice face broken to pieces, known only by a small mountain village in a time before cameras or livestreams or *Vogue*. So you took it for yourself, despite the rules. In any case, you haven't been docked for it yet.

Mahn Suk's face burns in your hands.

You stand. You wring your fingers, play with your joints. You've always enjoyed the pliability of human fingers—perfect for fidgeting with. You pop out your phalanges one by one and snap them back into place for the satisfaction. You do not need oxygen but you siphon breaths through the ornamental sacks you call lungs as you pace across the warehouse floor.

You decide to do what you do best: observe. You leave your meat behind and slip forward to the train station. Perched invisible, you watch the watery after image of yourself fading from the Continuity. It heals itself over as it always does—fills the gap you made in the crowd like a handprint in foam. You take in the ridiculous contortions of your face when you spotted the human—you watch yourself stumble and slip to the café.

You evaluate the human. They step off the train, a haggard commuter in a uniform, backlit by yellow light. They're nothing special, you conclude, then you convulse and snap past the surface tension of two hundred and sixty years so quickly that you spark like a neutron star. Raw with friction burns, you catapult into the warehouse, back into your meat, and roly-poly across the floorboards. You lie face down in a puddle of fluids escaping from every pore, suffused in a halo of steaming heat. Your appendix ruptures.

Love, yes. Perhaps. Love at first sight is the assumption that comes to mind, but there could be many other reasons for this crumpling, this flushing, *these liquids,* this irritating tide of hormones and gases and thermodynamics. After all, you had done a pretty shoddy job with your marrow and meat. Your hemoglobin isn't even the right shade—too pink. You also hadn't bothered with the proper folding between your gray and white matter and have to admit that it's mostly wet mush. Except for your amygdala. You make excellent amygdalas.

You must have forgotten to include receptors for essential hormones. Or added hormones humans aren't supposed to have. Maybe you triggered some spontaneous misfire, stimulants running haywire through this half-baked labyrinth you wear. That must be why you're nauseous, trembling. So are the molecules in the air. Why are they trembling too?

You realize you're screaming. You must have been screaming the entire time you fell. When you prop up your temporal gyrus (you have a habit of blocking out frequencies along the human-made range) the noise you're making is an unpleasant shrillness. Your vocal cords aren't any better made than the rest of you—you snip them and cough until they come fluttering out of your nostrils. They regrow within you like webs.

You step backward, out of the warehouse, and take a seat on a polar ice cap. Dry Antarctic winds wick away your soggy heat and you grow calm. It's easier to think under the midnight sun, just you, some distant penguins, and a glistening belt of ocean separating shore from sky.

Had there been anything anomalous at that train station? You recall the uncomfortable humidity, but it's always humid in human crowds: all the damp skin and orifices.

The train had been late. But then again, train lateness is only natural. You remember spending a boring afternoon watching the first coal-toting locomotive stall up a hill, shaking rickety in its wooden skeleton. And the hyperstellar railways of Capsula Nine miscalculate their gravitational dilation all the time, sometimes by decades.

Was it the smell then? You are sensitive to smells. But no, the air had smelled like mosquito wings and the soda lime glass of a million computer screens, as many cities do.

You think back to propping your mass between a ticket machine and the station wall, an exhausted commuter by all appearances. You had made a show of sifting through your briefcase on your knee. In reality, you had reached into a pocket dimension where you'd stored the human's biographical data recorded by your fellow Clerks (and what a mess: cuneiform stone tablets, subliminal messaging hidden in free-floating radio waves, copper engravings, floppy disks, hard drives, SD cards, the unraveled DNA of a Cuban sandwich, as well as stacks of loose college-ruled, A4, letter, legal, tabloid, cardstock, cotton, linen, birch bark, and pressed parchment papers in countless handwritings. You're only thankful the Repository refuses standardization "to preserve skew allotted by Clerk idiosyncracies." Whatever that means).

You had grasped a comprehensive yet lackluster record of a life: thirty-one, unpartnered, someone who had grown and worked in the same city from birth to present. A statistic. A human like any other human you had ever recorded. You thought such mundanity ironic, in light of the fact that their commute is the last moment to record in the entirety of Earthly existence—the final paragraph across the span of planetary history before The End of the World. In hindsight, perhaps a moment deserving gravitas if you cared about that kind of thing anymore.

You were supposed to describe their final moments: whether they scratched their nose or burped or checked their watch, their heart rate, their enzyme count, their last words. You'd done it countless times before. Then the Earth was supposed to turn to dust, taking them with it, and you were supposed to submit your final report before making an obligatory appearance at a work party on an asteroid greenhouse deep in the Andromeda Galaxy.

But then you *saw* the human and something overwhelming had happened inside you, your guts writhing like Monstrous Worms, and you'd gotten all weird and flung yourself through space-time to get away from that feeling. Twice. And now here you are, watching a distant colony of penguins squawk at their young.

You grab your briefcase, then step forward back to the café. For good measure, you twitch the Continuity threads so you have been at the window seat for the past half hour, a cronut in one hand and a magazine in the other.

You order a shot of espresso (technically your first, Continually your third) as you contemplate the possibility that maybe you are just tired. You have been tired for a very long time.

This reminder of your exhaustion sinks heavy in your chest (one of your porcelain ribs cracks). You need a vacation so badly that the very thought of it fills your mouth with water. After the End of the World, you fully intend on detaching from the Repository's ever-demanding attention and sinking into the folds of the universe's expansion, burrowing into a place where nobody can bother you for a good long while.

Whenever your fellow Clerks ask how you're going to spend your time off, you lie. You say you're going to dally on post-colonized Mars—a time of lawless risks under dusky orange skies, heated moments of passion in the sticky warmth of storm shelters, young bodies seeking meaning in the unknown, all the racketed substances a civilization could taste, and none of the bureaucracy.

Every assignment you've spent there has been a perfectly customized torture, not that you'd ever admit it. Most of your coworkers adore the human race and all its pleasures. They spend their free time (and much of their working time, you note with displeasure) ingratiating themselves to every sensational whim: tactile ardor, abuse of their synapses, succulent sensory delights. Humanity's cravings in a range of flavors you've never had a taste for.

You have to admit you're a bit odd, even by Clerk standards, but you also know fully well that there's a line between "eccentric odd" and "doesn't-get-invited-to-work-parties odd" that you haven't crossed yet and aren't keen to.

Besides, it's not like you hate humans. Far from it. For all your complaining, you admit you even like the Earth reasonably, although it's undeniably overhyped for being The One That Started It All. In your regard, others too often forget that it is the only macroecosystem to independently manifest such unpleasant things as hurricanes and mosquitoes and plague. Especially when you need to occupy a human body, you much prefer the sanitized biomes of the thousands of civilizations that will rise and fall after The End of the World.

No. It's not the Earth and it's not humans personally, but humans are sentient creatures and you've had more than your fill of sentient company. Your coveted plan is to spend the next few centuries buried as a crab on a Teegardian beach. You've even gone so far as to sculpt the mottled gray shell, sitting in your pocket, ready for donning the moment you clock out.

Your fingertips trace the carapace. You close your eyes. You take a final bite of your cronut and lean forward back onto the train station. You sit on a bench a full minute before The End of the World.

What is falling in love anyway? You hardly know. You are only capable of making assumptions from secondhand observations. Your previous assignment had been a prostitute in Damascus in AD forty-five, the one before that, a tech juggernaut monopolizing a nexus station between star systems. Both had many lovers, in the carnal sense, even in the open emotional sense, and all of it had been a kind of love in a way—maybe not always a love for their partners but a love for company at its simplest, and a love for power at its most fundamental. You remember a lot of it involving hunger. And manipulation. And secrets; you particularly remember the secrets.

You wonder what pulled you to that moldy warehouse—is it an instinct etched into your artificial DNA? Your shoddy-slapped genes urging you to procreation and the promised immortality of a new generation? Or is it loneliness?

A yawning commuter joins you on your bench. They pull a device out of their pocket and swipe through media blasted at full volume.

You rupture both ear canals on instinct, then reluctantly rebuild them. No, you are not lonely. Far from it. Teegarden is a planet without sentient life, its prokaryotes untouched by the roiling chaos cocktail of evolutionary progression. You long for this solitude to the point of pain (another rib snaps). You would do anything to be there now, hidden in your granular cloister, clawed, stiff, twitching, and the only complex organism across several thousand parsecs.

This weakness, this hesitance, is an error, you conclude. A symptom of anticipation. Not love then, just the thing that you thought human love was supposed to feel like. You make a note to be more careful with your marrow and meat next time.

A vibration from the speakers heralds the train's arrival. You move to the edge of the station platform, fiddling with your briefcase, counting the nanoseconds, waiting for the human to hurry up and get off so the World can End, and you can finally slip off your itchy flesh cage.

The train arrives, and the human steps onto the platform. You ready your ballpoint pen and your yellow notepad.

The human has blue hair, a popular trend for their era and not all that uncommon. They hustle off the train, head bent, brow furrowed, thrown by the tide of disembarkers. They have dark eyes, a warm complexion corrugated with acne, and wear silver Hublink piercings, marking them for a career in any one of the towering clusters of lights that make up the city. They clutch an umbrella although it hasn't rained that day.

This is as far as you can observe before you are in a Babylonian tomb, this time having thrown yourself so violently that you smash a line of ceramic urns and shatter your collarbone. You wheeze; your alveoli erupt in popcorn bursts.

The umbrella. It has to be the umbrella. You lie feverish, mind churning. You are reacting to the strangeness of the umbrella. But no, not that strange really. The sky had been gray that morning.

What is it then? What is this? You put a shaking hand to your chest then remember that you had forgotten to grow a heart. You make one now, shoving aside your shrunken spinal column. It takes less than a second to grow. It is a small misshapen pouch of toughened muscle with too many valves and an upside-down aorta, but it's functional. You search for your pulse as you concentrate on your prospective vacation. You think of the vibrations of a tide over your shell, a sepulcher incubating you in a salty mire. Your giddy heart thumps faster.

Then you think about the crown of a head shining cobalt in the harsh station lights, a widow's peak framed by flyaway strands, a hand clutched around an umbrella, a shadowed face lowered to the ground. Your rate goes tachycardic, you choke, and your heart palpitates itself into a dead lump.

You hunch over and convulse from your chest until you regurgitate the organ into your palm in a splatter of rosy fluid. You crush it into a carbon atom, wipe your mouth, then lower yourself into the dust to grow a new one.

You bend over the railing of an enclosure alight with the shifting hues of zooluminescent tardigrades—you sink into a velvet seat overlooking act two of *La Traviata*—you squat in a children's sandpit under a maple tree. Then you seat yourself on the edge of the International Space Station, purveying the remains of the Dead Planet Earth below.

You decide that you are confused, but you don't like that, so you decide that you are angry. It doesn't feel fair to be angry with the human—especially a human at The End of the World. You want to be angry with yourself, but crabs can't be angry. Crabs can't be bothered with anything, especially not crabs balanced on the cusp of cool tide and the warmth of three suns. No, you need to practice a crab state of being. Non-feeling. Complete objectivity.

Fuck Admin.

It's their damn fault. You leap at this revelation and land in a rice paddy, letting the cool mud soak into your shoes, your socks, and your thirteen toes. Yes, everything went wrong the moment they disrupted the neat linear records you and the other Clerks had maintained since the Beginning. Admin had abruptly decided to redo it all from scratch, demanding a new series of chronicles separated by "major historical turning points." Such a decision constituted a furious departmental discussion; after all, what the fuck is a "major historical turning point?"

You believed it asinine from the start. Admin did not invite you to their conversations (they never do—as they say, Clerks are recordkeepers, not decision makers), but you still argued, any opportunity you had, that history is not a conveniently mapped roadway, but an unpredictable wilderness of amalgamated microdecisions, some quite insignificant in scope, but no less important to the delicate ecosystem that defines the Present.

Many of your fellow Clerks protested as well, not so much for the sanctity of the work, but in indignation at the extra labor thrust upon you all. But Admin mentioned something about the preservation of the records and necessary security measures and taking extra precautions against the army of Monstrous Worms, who despise the Repository and would stop at nothing to invade and swallow it whole, thereby sweeping the very memory of humankind into an eternal nonexistence, etcetera, etcetera.

Then they said they were going to assign extra overtime to those who wouldn't stop complaining, which more or less got everyone in line.

You rolled your eyes (whenever you had any), watching Admin hold a millennium's worth of debates before they finally agreed on three "major turning points":

1. **The Creation of the Universe.** Invalid, you cried, as it was not a turning point at all. Just the beginning of The Point. There was nothing interesting to record in that relentless darkness before Time began. Except the cosmic battles against the Monstrous Worms, but who cares about those anymore?
2. **The First Sentient Creature.** Sure, you were there for that, but you did not believe it to be very special. The Creature had mostly used that sentience to make bad art and get better at killing things.

31

And of course,

3. **The End of the Planet Earth**—when an undiscovered classification of Higgs boson comes into existence in a faulty particle accelerator—eliciting a "Eureka!" from a collection of politicians, generals, and PhDs—before subsequently decaying every molecule on the planet Earth into oblivion.

This, you admit, is a dramatic event, but not one constituting a turning point. Turning implies change. A pivot. You tried demonstrating this several times to Admin, in a variety of forms, but Admin has not taken physical forms since the Dawn of the Cosmos. They had long-forgotten everything about the function of Euclidean space, including knowledge of pivoting. They do not remember that change implies a passing from one state to another: to difference. To entropy. When they dismissed you, you screamed long and hard into a black hole.

You scream now, stamping into the shallow water and flecking yourself with chaff. A family of water buffalo turns their heads to you.

Of course, this was all back when you still cared enough to argue that The End of the Planet Earth was neither the End of the Universe, nor the end of humankind. Sure the Earth crumbled into a dead gray thing, but the off-world humans made efficient work of containing the decay before it spread further. And that just catalyzed the whole lot to expand farther into the galaxy, upon which the species did rather well for themselves in the long run. You gave it a lot of thought in those early days. You even wrote a proposal suggesting that the turning points be divided as such:

1. **The First Egg Birth.** Catalyzing the gene-protecting maternal instinct that laid the primal bedrock of existence seemed, in your regard, much more important than a smooth-brained air breather having a thought.
2. **The First Seasoned Dish.** It had been a pounded animal thrown over embers, topped with mustard stems contributed by a pre-human with a sensitive nose and an anomalous neural pathway that would later evolve into a creative instinct. You had snatched some from the coals, then spit it out because it was too gamey. But it wasn't about the taste. It was about the smiling and the way they crouched closer to the fire to stick greasy handfuls in each other's faces and laugh over the bitterness of the char, the spicy note in each dripping mouthful. It was the way the little siblings danced out again in the muggy spring to gather more stems.

And,

3. **The First War**. It had been a small one centuries before the first human city laid its foundation. You do not remember much about how it started. But you never forgot their faces: the way the humans had looked at each other when dust settled over the gore oxidizing in pits of mud. Those expressions were not the last of their kind by a long shot, but they were the first. Those rigid faces, the smell penetrating the stillness, and the way they dragged their dead friends into the night sticks in your mind as mattering much much much more than the End of the Planet Earth.

Earth, Earth, the overrated Earth.

You can no longer bother yourself with an abstract council who impart their authority by function of boiling longer in the primordial soup, who haven't talked to a single human in eons, who don't even remember what a *pivot* is, going about it all wrong. You learned that your job is to record and observe and stay silent. All that matters is that the stupid new transition system requires centuries of overtime from each stupid Clerk in the Repository, to record ten billion stupid Last Days before the Earth Dies.

But back to love. First love on a train station, fifteen seconds before the irrevocable mass decay of the planet.

You lean back into a producer's chair. You watch young actors in period garb swoon in front of a green screen. You drink a kale smoothie.

Clearly, something is compromising your ability to perform your job. You consider trading your assignment. But even unofficial trades need a good reason behind them, and this isn't a good reason at all.

Your peers won't understand your distress. Your peers love love and all its rituals. In fact, if there were real career consequences for every salacious controversy of a Clerk getting too involved with a human, there wouldn't be enough Clerks to do shit.

You know it never matters. Your kind cannot indent the fabric of the Continuity in any significant way, nor can you leave any mark on human memory. You are forgotten in a head turn, a distraction, a blink.

Even now, as you wander onto the stage set, criticizing the inaccuracy of the costumes, rearranging the props, flinging smoothie everywhere, you know that they will not remember you in the next second, that these perplexed humans will go back to their scene and forget you as a hot stone forgets a wet handprint, as wet sand forgets a hot handprint, as the expensive lens will forget your fingerprint, drawing an oily smiling face on a camera that cannot see or retain you.

The appeal never made sense. Why chase these fleeting moments of intimacy when they vanish quicker than fog in sunshine? It seems debasing, more so than remaining faithful to your place in the peripheries.

These are the odd opinions you do not voice.

So a trade won't make sense to any of the others, and honestly doesn't make much sense to you. You slide back to the café, resolving that you want to do this. You want to get off this planet and be done with this pointless assignment so you can be a crab and not be bothered with hearts or lungs or Mahn Suk's slight overbite or the sticky damp or watching your fellow Clerks dance into endless forgotten nights.

You try again. A shot of espresso for luck, then back to the train station. Fifteen seconds. The End of the World approaches. So does the human.

Silver piercings. Chapped lips. Uneven bangs and those endless dark eyes. This time they almost meet your gaze and when you slip backward, you fall into a badger hole. You fracture your ankle.

You stand in a sorghum field in a place that will someday be a town, that will someday be a city. You groan and pinch yourself, then forget you didn't give yourself nerve endings so you grow nociceptors under your cheeks and slap yourself until you feel calmer.

Maybe it's Mahn Suk, you think. Maybe you copied more than just his nice symmetrical face. Maybe Mahn Suk, the drowned Joseon bronze apprentice, would have had a thing for blue hair if he had lived in a different time, a different place.

You don't want to take chances so you use the reflective surface of a duck pond to adjust yourself. You prod your brow, widen your cheekbones, indent your chin, scour your scalp, and take a foot off your spine for good measure. When you step back onto the station, you are a strange little thing.

Too little. The crowd jostles you forward, you lose your footing, and a child collides with you as she dashes out of her mother's grasp. You flatten instantly, toppling into someone else.

The mother rushes out, apologies dribbling down her chin. You read her microexpressions: embarrassment, followed by the masked curiosity humans put on when confronting unattractive members of their species, followed by a more profound embarrassment. You regret the duck pond.

The child asks something honest ("Why are his lips so *lumpy*, Mummy?"), and then they're whisked away, and you are still on the ground, and there is something warm moving underneath you.

You shift aside and catch a glimpse of blue hair, an umbrella cast askew, your chest on their shoulder, their knee prodding into your stomach, you on top, them below, that human, your human, you two tangled on the ground, *touching.*

When you get to your feet, you have one foot in a diplodocus nest. You strain your lower back, trying to keep your balance so you do not flail into the eggs. The herd bleats in reptilian fury as they stampede from the marsh.

You jump onto a sill eight hundred meters up the Burj Khalifa, swipe a fern off your shoe, then adjust yourself in the polished window. You add the foot back to your spine. You melt your face into a puddle that pools gooey pink into your hands then pinch it back together with your fingers, sculpting by instinct. Wind whistling in your ears, you stare at your reflection, and Mahn Suk's damned face stares back.

You give up and freefall. You do not return to the train station, but to a greenhouse one thousand years into the future and ten thousand lightyears away. You walk, with purpose, down ivy-strewn pathways soaked in the radiation of six moons. Coppery light bathes trees and shrubs, the last of their kind, all obscured in a pastel explosion of crepe paper party streamers.

"Hey!" the Clerks call. They're all human, you note with a twinge of disappointment. No chlorophyll or tentacles or fur or wings or carapaces—no third eyes or sixth fingers or so much as an unattractive face. *Where's the fun in it all?* you think glumly. Then again. Here you are looking like Mahn Suk.

"Nearly done?" one approaches you, and you do not recognize the body but you recognize the way they wear it.

"I like the new look," you comment. Small talk.

"Thanks. Hey. Your report's not in yet. We've got a fun kickoff for when you ship it to the Repository," they jerk their thumb at a goliath disco ball strung over the walkway. "It's filled with glitter and plasma. The fractals shatter into a mirror-tile dance floor when it falls. Pretty snazzy. We drop it when you're done." They purse their lips. "So why are you here if you're not done?"

"I've got a—situation," you say, and you contort Mahn Suk's face into an expression of blithe vulnerability. "Can you keep a secret?"

"Oh, of course," they say gutturally, because all Clerks love secrets.

"I think I may have fallen in love. With a human," you whisper. You hesitate and clarify, "The one I'm supposed to record."

They get so excited that they decompose in front of you, makeup and epidermis and oily adipose sloughing, then they bring themself back together with a clap of two perfectly manicured hands.

"Wonderful! Wonderful!" they exclaim. "We almost lost hope in you. Finally fell off your high cow didn't you?"

"Horse," you correct, because odd eccentrics are also notorious know-it-alls. "I need some advice if I'm going to get my report in. My physical reaction is so strong I can't get the last fifteen seconds."

"Can't omit that," they say seriously. "Almost got booked with double overtime when I submitted a report with six seconds missing. Accidentally missed one of five thousand and fifty-eight snores on a summer night. They're taking this new transition very seriously. And you're the tail of it all."

"Yes," you say, thinking longingly of tails and running free without so much as a stitch of clothing or a thought of trains. "So you see my problem. What do I do?"

They click their teeth in sharp short snaps before musing, "Have you tried interacting with the poor thing?"

"A little," you say. "I fell on them."

"And?"

"That's it."

"Okay. Why don't you try going further? Catch them a decade before their cells fall apart. Woo them. Stalk them. Do something charming with those pretty eyes you're wearing. Approach them in a moment of desperation. Etch your smile into a déjà vu familiarity. Stage serendipitous meetings. Maybe save their life a few times in increasingly fashionable outfits. When you're finally tired of that, then get back to that train station, get those fifteen seconds, and finish your report so you can join us."

They muse to themselves.

"You could go on for a few decades or so at least and be back before we bring out the canapes."

"But," you protest, and you want to say *I'd rather be swallowed by a Monstrous Worm than do all that*, but then you remember the line between the different types of odd and you finish, "That's not professional."

They sigh.

"I suppose. Physical reaction? It's miserable, isn't it?"

"Yeah," you say, "Especially the screaming."

They blink.

"What screaming?"

"I fell in love, then my body screamed."

"Your body isn't supposed to do that. Falling in love doesn't make you scream."

36

"Doesn't it?"

Doesn't it? Hadn't that prostitute in Damascus screamed by lamplight while soaking her cot in tears? And hadn't that tech juggernaut also screamed, red-faced, hands hard and eyes harder? Hadn't they both dealt in love, traded it in their business and absorbed it each night?

But your friend shakes their head, taps their manicure, and says, "No odd duck, why in the name of Death Earth would you scream when experiencing something so wonderful?"

Had it been wonderful? You can't tell. Watching the first egg-mother nuzzle its pearl of a genetic package into the crook of her limb—that had been wonderful. Dancing with children by the firelight while waiting for their meal to cook, slapping their siblings with branches—that had been wonderful. The strained grunts as men carried men off a battlefield, cleaning the dirt off each other's faces and gluing down souls with nothing but prayers and rags—that too, had been wonderful in its own way. And terrible. All of it had also been so terrible. But wasn't that the point?

"There was a lot of sweating," you add. "And shaking. And itching. It was hard to breathe."

"Sounds like an allergy," they wrinkle their nose. "Did you tamper with your mast cells? You know that's not allowed, right?"

You didn't tamper with your mast cells because you forgot to make any at all.

"It's not an allergy."

"Huh," they cock their head. "Maybe it isn't love. Maybe you're just stressed. Or you developed some obsessive attachment to this assignment and don't want it to end."

Well, that isn't right. You flip the crab shell in your pocket over and over between your fingers.

"I should get back."

"You should. It's just fifteen seconds, darling. Where are you going to settle after the party?"

"Mars," you say, and you step back onto the train station, sitting on a bench next to a human watching videosat maximum volume.

You wait. You quiet your breathing. Your heart beats, steady, slow, synchronized.

The human arrives.

A wetness in your palms and a dryness in your mouth, and your molecules straining to be anywhere else, but you screw yourself where you are (literally—you twist the fibers of your soles down deep into the concrete) and force yourself to keep your eyes trained on them as you ready your pen. The humidity. The temperature. Their microexpressions.

Fifteen. Fourteen. Thirteen.

They see you. You make eye contact across a disembarking crowd. You are half submerged in the slipstreams—you feel a warm breeze on the back of your neck, swirling with long-extinct microbes, but you do not jump, you do not step away. You force yourself into this present, mustering an impartiality worthy of pincers and an exoskeleton. So what if their eyes are deep and black and bottomless as the Beginning of the Cosmos? So what if there's something predatory—something hungry in the slow grin creeping across their face as you lock gazes?

Twelve. Eleven. Ten.

You are shaking; you are dying. Your heart churns itself into a violence. You are a color no human should be, trembling and palpating, so much that your bench companion side-eyes you in a panic and begins typing in a number for emergency services. The human—your human—brushes a strand of blue hair out of their face and begins to move toward you.

You want nothing more than to run. You are a faithful Clerk. You are combusting. You write. It is horrible torture, but it is your job, and you really really need a vacation.

Nine. Eight. Seven.

Those eyes. That build. Average size, shape, health. Average upbringing, education, job. A perfect median amalgamation, odd in and of itself for after all, aren't they all irritatingly distinct in their own way? That's why your job exists. The preservation of all those entropic lives. Is it the averageness you love? The novelty of it?

Is it even love? Why did you scream? You feel another noise rising, like sour bile in your throat, and you collapse your larynx to stifle it.

They continue to smile at you, a perfect average human expression, not too wide, not too soft, and the rest of your insides fully implode. You stand upright by sheer willpower, every cavity within you hollow and smoking. Why aren't they leaving? Why are they coming toward you? The tide of commuters eddies around them like a current around an approaching alligator.

Six, five, four.

You're almost done. You scratch your last remarks, noting now the angle of their posture, the staccato tapping of their umbrella against their thigh, and their final act— reaching out toward you. Toward your briefcase.

Then you think, *Shit.*

They are close enough for you to feel the heat of their breath, to count the threads in their shirt.

I'm the last Clerk.

You clench your gummy fists. Something is wrong, something is off, and it's not just you, falling apart.

I'm the last one. And then—Oh. Oh no—

Three. Two. One—

You leap into a stretch of cosmic void. The nearest star is so far away that it provides neither a newton of gravity nor a photon of light. You are drowned in complete and utter darkness.

You dissolve your body and now float, peeled and vulnerable, as your true self, no Mahn Suk face to hide behind. You are pure energy, a mind and a soul, now divorced from the molecular obligations of your meat.

You are not alone. When the human grabbed your briefcase, you dragged them from the train station. You feel the pressure of their flesh unspooling in the void.

Then a voice croons, *I can swallow you. I can swallow you now.*

And it can. A Monstrous Worm can swallow anything. It eats and eats and is never sated because it craves the Repository above all else—to digest the record of human existence. It salivates now—pure appetite and desire dripping in waves through you.

If you were still in a human body, it would have stiffened, hair shock-white, a rigor mortis clench cracking every tooth in your jaw. But you've discarded your marrow and meat. You touch your emotions raw with blissful clarity.

Fear, not love. For all your half-assery, you had a functioning amygdala. It's the only tissue you can make perfectly, without thought. Admin trained you to this extent—make an amygdala, then build everything else around it. Be alert, be vigilant, because a Monstrous Worm will stop at nothing to exploit you—to manipulate and wheedle until it finds its feast.

"You must be deadly afraid," they instructed you when you were a fresh idiot. "So afraid that you will recognize one in any form it takes. Be as afraid of it as humans are of the dark, of the unknown."

And of course it had taken a median amalgamation. What better way to get lost in a record? It had infested a host so very mundane, so very ordinary—worked, lived, melted into a backdrop of human white noise—because it knew you all would be watching. Observing every moment. Recording. And that each datum would accumulate, expound on the next, passed from Clerk to Clerk until the final moment—the completed record sent directly to the Repository.

It would have latched to your report. It would have clenched ahold of your final submission, and the length of the Monstrous Worm would have slipped away from the Earth's destruction and siphoned directly into the heart of the Repository. It would have swallowed Admin first, then ravaged every carefully separated encyclopedia. And its other end—its other mouth, you realize, it would have tethered to *you* as you rejoined your coworkers at their garden party—and it would have made a feast of all of you too, cracked open your human shells and slurped you all, soft and slithering, down its immortal gullet.

Except that didn't happen. You had caught that alligator smile, that overeager hand, and brought it here, to a useless, lifeless corner of the universe. It is furious. It snaps up your briefcase.

The Monstrous Worm has no eyes and cannot see or be seen, but even in this absolute nothingness, it has a gaze that it turns in full force upon you. The wrath, the famine, of its attention is enough to wither you where you are. You—intangible, massless, flayed to your core, alive and yearning for rest.

You want to be a crab.

You will be digested for an eternity.

The Monstrous Worm howls a terrible song—the same song it sang into battle at the beginning of the universe.

The Monstrous Worm opens its mouth.

The Monstrous Worm embraces you with its Monstrous Tongue.

Then it screams.

A flash pierces the endless night—something bright harpoons the Worm's interior and pins it, writhing and dying, to a locus.

A second later, you realize that Admin had suddenly appeared, towing a young star in their wake. They had condensed the immensity of the star's nuclear gravity into a vector and shot it directly down the Monstrous Worm in a blazing fury.

For a horrible moment, you see it illuminated in all its unfathomable hideousness—its galactical jaws widened over you—the infinite tortures that would have awaited you down the length of its throat.

But then it crackles, and implodes, and the tongue slackens around you and you hunch over as one of Admin's many Hands grabs you, stuffs you into a body, and sends you to a Singaporean food market.

The night is damp, the chair is plastic, and your hands are curled around a foam tray topped with mei fun. Compared to the silence of the void a split second ago, the buzz of the market blasts like a shotgun into your skull.

A Hand of Admin sits across from you, dressed in a track jacket and a fur cap. Their face is stiff, like the uncracked spine of a book, the shadows and crevices folded wrong, the hair a tad too plastic.

"We haven't taken a physical form in eons," they say redundantly. "Does it look alright?"

You nod. You quiver. The weight of your cheeks and the chattering teeth in your mouth are familiar. Somehow, you have Mahn Suk's face again.

"Right, so," the Hand works their fingers around a pandan tea and sips between words. "It took a little longer than we expected, but good work. We have dispatched the Worm and erased all evidence of it from the Continuity. The human it took as a host will need new documentation, of course—but we can have the younger Clerks get it done. They need the practice. This liquid is very saccharine."

They set the cup down.

"Do you have any questions before your temporary leave of absence? You've been promoted. To Head Clerk. Catch us another Worm, and we might promote you to Admin by the end of the millennia."

"I—" your voice cracks. You push noodles into your mouth, and the taste shocks you to the reality of your survival. A snow pea falls from your lips, and your meat begins to cry.

The Hand watches. You wonder if they know what it is you're doing, if they're merely waiting as one would wait for someone to stop coughing.

"Did you," you finally warble. "Use me as *bait*?"

"Of course not," they scoff. "We noted your penchant for keen observation in past reports and decided that you, of all the Clerks, would be most capable of ascertaining the true nature of a Worm in its disguise. The transfer of records is a most vulnerable moment for invasion. We gave you this assignment deliberately, knowing that the Worms would take advantage of our new classification system to breach the Repository. We were merely uncertain which epoch they would deem most opportune. Without due vigilance, we would have been completely helpless to its appetite. However, true to our expectations, you posed a tempting target. You had the instincts to isolate it to a secondary location, which allowed us to dispatch it once it exposed itself."

Admin doesn't know what fishing is.

"What about the human?" you ask. A parasite's mask. A human life stolen to lull invisible observers into a false sense of security. How long did it live in that stolen flesh? Two hours? Two days? From birth? You speculate in despair; from *birth*? You feel a sickness in your upper abdomen, which is your first clue that this is a truly well-made body.

The Hand taps the table. You can see their features elongating ever so slightly as they shift under their skin. They're trying to smile, you realize.

"Since we have expunged all traces of the Worm from the Continuity, it never technically took a host. The End of the Planet Earth will proceed, and said former host represents the last documentation needed before we focus our efforts on the next chronology. As stated, the new Clerks can take this assignment. It'll be good for them."

In another place and another time, you know, an average human with dark eyes dreams of exploding in a void.

"Congratulations," they say as they stand. "We felt this accomplishment was deserving of a corporeal greeting."

They stand utterly still for a moment with their rubbery face contorting pre-sneeze—and you do not blame them because the courtyard is thick with smoke from heated oil, soy sauce, garlic, onion, chili, butter, and curry powder, cut through with the overpowering smell of cicadas and human sweat.

Around you swim hundreds of conversations in a dozen languages which you card through like tangled wool—around you are hundreds of humans unaware that every passing second of their lives has been carefully observed, recorded, and categorized. They do not realize that the details of their existence make up the fabric of reality, that it all matters so much.

"Why didn't you tell me any of this?" you ask.

"When do Clerks ever listen to us?" comes the wry reply.

Admin slips away. You take fifteen minutes to finish the mei fun and the abandoned tea. While you do, you fashion a new carapace.

You push aside your tray and put your head on the table. The table becomes sand and the chatter becomes tide and the night sky above you collapses into a salt-rich ether. You slip away to a beach on Teegarden, where you are the only sentient being across several thousand parsecs.

You use your pincers to carve a tunnel into the shore. You burrow. You are small, safe, and suctioned within the rhythm of a thunderous tide. Cool damp seeps from below, the warmth of three suns from above.

Peace at last. It takes you a year to get comfortable, another twenty to process your emotions enough to fully enjoy each slow, calm moment.

Somewhere far away in time, you know your fellow Clerks drop a disco ball that shatters into a perfect fractal dance floor. They note your absence and comment on your oddities. They may not believe you are capable of love. But you know you are because there is love here in your shell, savoring the sensation of being alive. There was love in your sculpted face, in your collapsing construct of feelings and meat, in your resolve while you stared down the maw of an ancient devourer. It is for love that you will return to your work, why you will, someday, extricate yourself from the sand, and step forward into another humid crowd. Uncomfortable, yes. Misshapen and anomalous and yearning. They will pass you by as a forgotten stranger, and you will preserve them in the crook of their mothers' elbows, in the heat of their meals, in their blood and loss. All those entropic lives.

ABOUT THE AUTHOR

H.H. Pak is a Los Angeles-born child of Korean immigrants and a strong believer in the power of sacrificial love. When they are not working towards their aspirations in the medical field or co-editing for *Wyrmhole Magazine,* they dream about space operas, make cringe art, and bother their dog too much.

Understudies
GREG EGAN

1

"It's completely up to you, whether you want to go ahead with this," Vince's father said, looking almost as uncomfortable as Vince in the sound-deadening, white-carpeted waiting room. "Maybe it would help you with your schoolwork and open up more choices in the long run. But it's your choice what you do right now."

"Did I do badly on the test?" Vince asked. On his last visit to Dr. Meadows, he'd tried to stay focused as he worked through the interminable list of logic puzzles and word games she'd given him, but they were the kind of thing where one or two at a time were fun, but after that, it was hard to keep his mind from wandering.

"We're not supposed to tell you your score," his father replied. "If it's too high, it could make you complacent, and if it's too low, it could make you feel bad."

"Does that mean you can tell me if it was just right?"

Vince's father looked confused. "No," he decided. "Otherwise, not telling you would tell you that it wasn't."

Dr. Meadows opened the door to her office. "Please come in."

Vince did his best to hide his impatience while she re-explained the principles of the device, as if the fact that he wasn't yet using it meant he couldn't possibly recall what she'd said to him the last time. When she finally asked him to take off his own glasses, and she pried the new ones out of their sleek black case, he caught the glorious factory-fresh smell of them and had to force himself not to laugh.

"These transducers generate the ultrasound that will stimulate your olfactory nerves," she said, pointing to tiny silver rectangles on the nose pads. "Let's try some calibrations first."

He accepted the glasses from her and put them on. The lenses matched his prescription, and the frames didn't feel any heavier than usual. He doubted anyone at school would even notice the change.

Dr. Meadows thumbed through an app on her phone, then tapped something on the screen. "Can you describe what you're smelling?" she asked.

"Vanilla." Vince did laugh now; it was insane how convincing the illusion was—as believable as the outgassing plastic in the glasses themselves.

"And now?"

"Toast."

"Is it burned?"

"I don't think so." Vince's mouth was watering slightly; the scent was so real that he could imagine butter melting through the crisp brown surface into the soft bread below. Before, he'd wondered why they'd never made movies that used this trick, but now it seemed obvious that it would be too distracting.

"Now?"

"Some kind of flower. I don't know the name."

Then a whiff of ammonia. The stench of burning tires. Vince hoped these crude notes were just mapping the farthest corners of his olfactory gamut, planting signposts in the badlands that he'd never have to visit again.

"All right." Dr. Meadows put down her phone. She led Vince through to the room where he'd sat for his previous assessment; the same tablet computer was waiting for him on the desk.

"I'd like you to try to solve these puzzles," she said. "But it's important that you keep the glasses on while you work. How does that sound?"

"It's fine," Vince replied. Maybe the first test had measured some kind of baseline to help choose the problems he'd be confronted with now. But he guessed what mattered most was the effect the glasses would have, not on his current performance, but on the follow-up.

Dr. Meadows left him to it. The first puzzle involved a tangle of overlapping triangles, with the lengths of some edges marked and others to be found. Vince concentrated on the task, and it wasn't until he'd completed it that he even registered the subtle odor the glasses had been inducing while he worked, vaguely reminiscent of pencil shavings, with a hint of loam. But it was fading now, and as he started on the second problem, it was replaced by something more like orange peel and copper wire.

An hour later, Dr. Meadows returned, and Vince rejoined his father in her office. "Tonight, as you sleep, you'll need to wear a different set of transducers," she explained. She removed the second device from its packaging, and Vince tried it on; it was like a bandage stuck over the top part of his nose. "And this unit needs to sit by your bedside." She handed Vince's father a box the size of a small Wi-Fi router, with the manufacturer's name, Combray, embossed on the side.

In bed that night, Vince barely felt the tape against his skin, but he kept thinking about the software in the Combray box, a gargoyle squatting on his bookshelf just waiting for him to drift off so it could reach across the darkness and run a red correction pen through his dreams. Did he really want to spend the next four years reliving every lesson in his sleep? Until now, his dreams had been a glorious refuge from the tedium and mundanity of school life. If his mind wasn't free when he lay down and closed his eyes, when would it be?

But he needed this. His mother was unemployed, and his father was endlessly anxious, sure that he'd be made redundant any day now. Vince knew he was not exceptional, himself, in any way that he could imagine earning him an income. He needed some kind of advantage to have any hope of staying off the scrap heap. And of all the advantages money could buy, this seemed like the most honest: shoring up the foundations he was building for himself, by making his brain a little less eager to recycle every hard-won lesson into rubble.

In the morning, as soon as he woke, Vince knew that he'd dreamed about the puzzles he'd grappled with the day before. He'd followed the lengths and angles of a chain of triangles around a loop, until the implications came full circle and a single answer was revealed. But in the dream, the whole pursuit had left him feeling as triumphant as a hunter who'd just learned to corner an antelope—even if the odors evoked were milder and tamer than a terrified animal's sweat and dung. And later, he'd sketched Venn diagrams with all the care of a famished seed gatherer rehearsing the route to a newly found tree that would furnish his next ten meals. Everything the glasses had marked with their scent, and the gargoyle had summoned back into his mind, had become vivid, urgent, and indelible.

He climbed out of bed and walked down the hallway. In the kitchen, he poured a bowl of cereal and doused it with milk, leaving it to soak while he went to the toilet. It wasn't quite six in the morning, and his father's alarm clock had yet to go off.

Vince finished eating and returned to his room. There were three more weeks until the start of school. He recalled his uncle Benjamin—who had a Combray of his own, and had paid for the gift—musing about all the skills he might have baked into his brain over the summer holidays if he'd had the same mental ratchet as a teenager that he had now.

Vince picked up his tablet and opened the book of magic tricks he'd been browsing for the last few days, fascinated but not quite dedicated enough to commit to learning any of them. He wouldn't be returning to Dr. Meadows for the official verdict for another week, but the dreams already felt conclusive, and he might as well have some fun with the gargoyle before it became one more slave to the curriculum.

2

"Put as many pieces on the board as you like, wherever you want," Vince explained to the gathered circle of his friends. "I'll keep my back turned. Tell the board you're done, and it will remove one of the pieces or put a new one on an empty square. Then you get to change one more square yourself. When I turn around, I'll look at the board and tell you exactly which square you changed—even though I never knew how it looked before."

After some clarification of the rules, everyone agreed to them, though they were skeptical that Vince had any hope of success without cheating. Zach made him remove his glasses, and Mira checked that he wasn't wearing earbuds. "Turn off the Wi-Fi and Bluetooth on the tablet, if you like," Vince suggested, and Wahid took him up on that.

"Okay." Vince turned away, leaving them to slide pieces onto the virtual chessboard at will. When they tapped the "Done" button there would normally have been an acknowledging ping, but Vince had preemptively turned off the sound in case someone accused him of receiving a secret message encoded in the tone.

"Okay," Zach said. "We're finished, you can look."

Vince turned and examined the board, scanning it quickly and performing all the calculations he needed in his head. "Fourth row down, fifth column," he announced. "The last thing you did was adding that knight."

Zach laughed. "Not bad," he said begrudgingly.

"Yeah, but you must have cheated somehow," Leon insisted.

"Blindfold me," Vince offered. "Or I can go and stand twenty meters away."

"Why does the board get to change one of the pieces?" Mira asked suspiciously.

Vince smiled. "Those are the rules."

Just as he was about to step away and let his friends commence round two, he heard a hubbub from the other side of the quadrangle. He turned to see Jamie Mellick at the center of a small crowd of onlookers, apparently performing some kind of dance.

Vince hesitated, wondering if the most merciful thing would be to urge his friends to ignore the whole spectacle. Jamie was the most uncoordinated person Vince had ever met, and he didn't want them adding to the pile on of ridicule.

But as he stood listening to the response of the crowd, he realized that the shouts of admiration were not ironic. Nobody was laughing, or mocking Jamie; they were enraptured.

By now Vince's friends had already gone in for a closer look, so he picked up his tablet and followed them. He couldn't squeeze to the front of the crowd, but he found a vantage point where he could get a decent view.

Jamie was tap dancing on the concrete steps that led up to the platform at the end of the quad. Joyfully, energetically, tirelessly, and—though the rhythm was so complex it took Vince some time to be sure—flawlessly.

It was breathtaking. Tap wasn't an art Vince had any particular knowledge of or fondness for, but Jamie seemed to have mastered moves so exuberant and so wildly demanding that Vince could not imagine how he could have wrung more astonishment and exhilaration out of the audience, short of doing it all on the wing of a biplane.

When Jamie finally ended his routine, the audience cheered and applauded. And his timing was perfect on another count: seconds later, the siren sounded for the start of first period, sending everyone away with a smile on their face but no chance to mob him and beg for his secret.

Vince caught Jamie's eye and offered an admiring nod; Jamie beamed back at him, sweaty but elated. This was . . . *some special shit*, Vince was sure, but surely not a Combray. Jamie could have practiced all summer, ratcheting up his progress with hardwood-scented dreams, and still not mastered a fraction of the skill he'd just displayed.

But ten minutes into Vince's English class, someone had already solved the mystery, having found the video diary of a novice learning a different style of dance with the help of a rudimentary exoskeleton. Vince felt a momentary pang of disillusionment, but then, the diarist made it clear that you couldn't learn the moves the exoskeleton imposed on your limbs merely by surrendering to it like a rag doll. It let you experience certain aspects of what an accomplished performance would *feel like*—giving you a clear target to aim for with each individual muscle and joint, which was easier than trying to steer the process by watching yourself in a mirror—but it was still up to you to find your own way to match those internal perceptions once you were standing entirely on your own two feet.

"Now we'll parse this into subject and predicate," the avatar on the Shared Attention Screen at the front of the classroom continued. The supervisor, who'd been listlessly watching the class from her desk, rose and walked down the aisle—perhaps hoping to learn the source of the delight on so many of the students' faces—but the app they'd been using to share the exoskeleton video detected her gaze and fled into the background, leaving nothing for her to see but a neatly diagrammed sentence.

At lunchtime, Vince came clean to his friends, describing the calculations that let him identify the square they'd changed, once the board's own small intervention had guaranteed the right kind of baseline.

"How long did it take to learn to do that in your head?" Zach asked, still skeptical.

Vince said, "Half an hour a day, for three days. But my uncle bought me a Christmas present that helped me get more out of the practice sessions." He took off his glasses and pointed out the transducers, explaining their function.

Everyone seemed to find the prospect of lessons with a Smell-O-Vision track hilarious; Vince sat smiling as he waited for them to stop riffing off each others' fart jokes. "It does work, though," he said. "And nothing smells that bad. It's usually pretty low-key; the board trick smelled like some kind of dry leaves, but that was enough for me to pick up the trail."

"Can it teach you to dance like Jamie?" Mira asked.

"Probably not," Vince admitted. But any jealousy he'd felt had had time to fade, and in all honesty, it wasn't the kind of skill he'd ever wanted. "It's good to have both methods," he decided. "Different ways to get one over on the machines."

"You mean get one over on the people who don't have the same machines as you do," Leon corrected him. "It's just a different way of cheating, for people who can't afford a Cyrano."

Mira scowled. "Using scents as a cue isn't cheating. I color-code my notes; it's not that different."

Zach said, "My cousins both have Cyranos. When I call them, it's creepy as fuck; sometimes it takes me thirty seconds to figure out if I'm talking to a human or not."

"And how's what Jamie did all that different?" Leon persisted.

Mira said, "I'm pretty sure he wasn't still wearing his robot dance teacher under his jeans."

"So if I used a Cyrano for a couple of months, then stopped, that wouldn't be cheating?" Leon countered.

Wahid said, "People who use a Cyrano then stop usually end up worse than they started."

"What happens when your cousins sit for exams?" Vince asked Zach.

"They go to a private school that treats the Cyranos as part of the person," Zach replied. "They wouldn't expect you to switch it off in an exam, any more than they'd ask you to switch off a pacemaker."

"Okay . . . but when they get to university?"

Zach said, "A couple of universities have the same policy already. And five years from now, I think most employers will, too. Your job, your degree, your CV, will all belong to the pair, not the human alone."

"Wouldn't it be cheaper for companies to run their own AI, instead of hiring all that dead weight to lip-synch the answers?" Mira suggested.

"Depends on the job," Wahid replied. "There'll always be a few that can't be done that way, for customer appeal or legal reasons. And some where it's obvious an AI would be useless, but they'll still hire a human-Cyrano pair and claim that the Cyrano will make them more efficient."

Zach laughed. "I can already see my cousins' future: sleeping on the job or playing video games in their heads, while their bodies are just there to reassure people that there's a human in the loop."

3

"Things might be tight for a while," Vince's father said. "But we knew this was coming, so we've prepared for it as best as we can. I don't want you to worry."

The twins had gone to bed an hour before; Vince had been watching videos in his room, and he'd only come out to get a drink of water. But it looked like his parents had been waiting since dinnertime to find the right moment to give him the news.

"How can people not need plumbers?" Vince asked. "I never saw a robot that could change a washer."

"People still need plumbers," his father said. "Just not as many. In construction, there are more prefabricated units. In maintenance, one person can do more with the new tools. Robots can't change washers, but the burrowers can lay pipes, and the crawlers can clear blockages."

"What are you going to do?"

"I'll retrain."

"As what?"

"I haven't decided yet. But if it's a course that's on the list of skills shortages, I'll get a living allowance while I study, so that will help."

"You should take my glasses," Vince offered. "They'll make it easier."

His father smiled. "Thanks, but I'll be okay. I'm glad the glasses are helping you. Maybe I'll get my own pair."

Vince glanced at his mother, who'd been looking on in silence. She'd lost her job as a history teacher just after Carol and Ethan were born, and she'd studied for three years with the aim of becoming a lab technician in the mining industry. But she still hadn't found a position.

"I don't want you to be unhappy," Vince said.

His father laughed and shook his head, as if to dismiss the possibility, but he walked over to Vince and embraced him. "I told you not to worry!" he said. "It will all be fine."

4

Vince's marks climbed, but as the end of term approached, he found himself looking back on the ascent with a sense of anticlimax. He hadn't conquered anything difficult; he'd just organized his efforts a little better than before, and with the Combray's help, everything he'd studied had fallen into place. Maybe he could get straight As from here to the end of high school, and no doubt that would be better than failing. But would it really give him a chance to survive in the world, let alone achieve anything he could be proud of?

On the last day before the break, when the gang came together on the lawn at lunchtime, everyone seemed equally restless.

"I heard Jamie made three thousand dollars in two weeks," Mira said. "Busking in Central Station at rush hour."

"Good for him," Vince replied. No one would tip a robot's owner for a machine doing what Jamie did, let alone pay money to watch a deepfake, but a human in the flesh could still be astonishing. "He's found his thing."

"For now," Zach said. "People will get bored with it eventually."

"That's when Vince will swoop in and wow everyone with his magic," Wahid joked.

Vince laughed. "That's not going to happen." Of the half dozen tricks he'd learned, none had a payoff that came fast enough to make a weary commuter look twice.

"But if Smell-O-Vision is such a great superpower, why aren't you rich?" Leon taunted him. "Or did your uncle spend all that money just to give you a fancy version of color-coded binders?"

"Maybe I needed the fancy version," Vince conceded. "Not to get rich, just to stay in the race. But why are you giving me shit about it? Hyperfine Minds, who make the Cyranos, keep telling us they're changing the world for the better . . . but if that's true, why aren't we *all* rich?"

"Because that's beyond their powers," Leon replied. "Even if they wanted it."

Vince said, "Exactly. All they're really doing is clawing money out of terrified parents who think they're buying a future for their kids."

"But their kids *will* get the best jobs," Wahid predicted. "The hype's too big to fail. Every CEO and their dog have already declared that Cyranos will make the perfect workforce, tripling productivity and sending profits through the roof. Once you've written that into your earnings forecast, how do you back down?"

"So we're screwed," Mira said blithely. "Unless we can borrow Jamie's exo and get it to train us to be jewel thieves."

Vince couldn't retreat into breezy cynicism; everything cut too close now. He said, "What if all the hype is wrong? What if Cyranos don't make their partners any smarter, and the humans don't do much for the Cyranos either? There must be some way we can prepare for the moment when they start falling flat on their faces."

Zach frowned. "Prepare how?"

"We need to be waiting in the wings, ready to step in and take their place," Vince decided. "Ready to do what they promised but can't deliver."

Zach said, "If the companies have swallowed the hype, they might never admit that they were wrong. They might just keep the Cyranos and find a way to work around the damage."

Vince was undeterred. "Then we'll need to be a part of how they work around the damage."

Zach laughed uneasily. "You really want to pin your hopes on picking up the pieces from the great Cyrano crash? What if it happens before we've even finished high school? Or five years later? Or never?"

Vince thought for a while. "If it comes sooner than expected, that's great; that'll mean it was impossible to hide, and in the aftermath, there should be a chance for everyone."

"And if it doesn't come when you need it?" Zach pressed him.

Vince said, "Then we might have to give it a little push."

5

Over the break, Vince studied like never before. He looked up the curricula for all his courses for the rest of the year and worked his way through them, switching between subjects whenever he felt burned out, confident that he could pick up each thread again wherever he'd left off.

In the second week, he made the whole endeavor ten times easier by letting himself go off on tangents. The coursework itself was about as exciting as eating chalk, but much of it consisted of parts, however narrow, of larger bodies of knowledge that were packed with glorious puzzles and revelations. When the module on electricity threatened to extinguish every spark in his soul, Vince flew off for a day-long excursion into Faraday's insights and Maxwell's equations, the links to relativity, the quantum version, the unification with the weak force, and the role of the Higgs boson. He returned, giddy and elated, to find that most of what he'd been struggling to absorb was now obvious from the wider context.

"I hope you're playing games with your friends!" his father called to him through the door of his room. Vince didn't reply; it seemed wiser not to explain his ambitions. His father was also studying, retraining as a refrigeration engineer, in between shifts of work-for-the-dole graffiti removal for the local council.

Back at school, Vince kept up his schedule, wearing earbuds to block out the avatars' lectures, and sandboxing the tutor on his tablet with a loop of himself paying attention to its earnest explication of things he already knew. In reality, he'd moved on to the next year's topics, but he kept exploring an ever-wider swathe of the surrounding territory. Classroom tests and homework dragged him back, but between the scent trails that helped him reload old perspectives and the broader view that put the material in context, he rarely had trouble jumping through those hoops.

In the third week of term, Vince stayed late to finish a physics experiment—pretending he'd messed up his measurements of a simple RLC circuit, when he was really playing around with something more interesting. A bored supervisor watched videos on his phone while Vince's tutor babbled advice about checking the leads on the alligator clips. Eventually, the supervisor hit the ceiling on his overtime and put an end to the experiment.

As Vince left the school grounds, Zach caught up with him, having just finished two hours of swimming training.

"Have you been in detention?" Zach joked.

"No, I was trying to understand superheterodyne mixing."

"You were what?"

Vince gave up on the idea of keeping his new regimen secret. There was nothing he could say now that would make sense, short of disclosing the whole backstory.

"Okay," Zach said. "But where's this speedrunning every level of high school going to get you?"

"Level with the Cyranos, eventually."

Zach regarded him dubiously. "You know they can look up anything in a fraction of a second?"

Vince was unfazed. "So what? There aren't many jobs that depend on reciting who won every Oscar in 1963."

"They can also calculate faster than you," Zach added.

"Not much faster than me with a calculator or the right kind of mathematics software. You might as well say they can pick up a ten-ton weight by interfacing with a crane. Well, so can I, if I have the same access codes. It's the crane that's doing the work."

Zach's skepticism seemed to waver a little. "But Cyranos are still . . . shinier, buzzier. 'Human and AI, raised side by side, building on each other's strengths!'"

"I thought you said your cousins were lazy fucks who zone out in class and watch porn on their contact lenses while their better halves look up the answers on the net and treat them as ventriloquist dolls."

"Yes," Zach agreed, "but not all pairs are like that. I've met some of the other students at their school, and . . . "

"What?"

Zach seemed almost embarrassed, but he continued. "They were only a couple of years older than me, but listening to them talk, it was like they'd seen everything, read everything, traveled the world."

Vince said, "There's a reason they call them Cyranos. Did you ever really have a conversation that challenged them?"

"Yeah, I asked for their analysis of Kierkegaard's Ninth Symphony, while we played water polo in my uncle's pool."

Vince said, "I'll take that as a no."

"So what's the plan?" Zach asked. "Turn yourself into a scratch-and-sniff prodigy and go start a degree before you turn fifteen?"

"No. But we need to be able to show up the Cyranos, to prove that we're their equals, or better."

Zach nodded. "That shouldn't be too hard. So . . . will you challenge them at Jeopardy, chess, or Go?"

"I don't know what their weakness is, yet," Vince admitted. "But from the studies I've read, it's not just freeloaders like your cousins who end up losing their edge. Everyone 'offloads some competence' and gets worse at some tasks."

"Yeah, but how does that help?" Zach asked. "You don't get to unplug the Cyrano and leave the human stumbling around like a hiker who's lost GPS."

"GPS is pretty reliable," Vince mused. "But if the map itself is wrong, you don't need to lose the signal to end up in a ditch."

Zach said, "Okay. Good luck turning that metaphor into an actual strategy." They'd reached the corner where they went different ways; he raised a hand in farewell, and they parted.

6

When Vince applied for a meeting with the school's head supervisor and chose the subject "Extracurricular Activities" from the drop-down menu, he was not optimistic. But he received a reply just two hours after completing the request, and his appointment was the very next day.

Mr. Randall welcomed Vince into his office and got straight to the point. "What did you have in mind?"

"An interschool academic challenge," Vince replied. "Between the six schools in the area, like we do with sports." They were all public schools, devoid of Cyranos, but he couldn't approach the enemy directly; he had to start by laying down the bait.

"So . . . a general knowledge quiz? A debate? Model United Nations? Mathematical Olympiad?"

Vince said, "The coolest thing right now is called an Adversarial Quiz. Each team gets to choose the questions that their opponents have to answer."

Mr. Randall was wary. "How is that fair? You could ask something impossibly hard, or something you could only know yourselves."

"If you think a question's unfair, you can always challenge it," Vince replied. "It mustn't rely on secret knowledge or some huge prior effort; the questioners need to be able to show how to reach the answer with just a few minutes' work, starting from facts that are well known among their peers."

"Who decides what is or isn't 'well known'?"

"There's a panel of three adjudicators for each match, drawn from the other schools in the competition. And if there's any favoritism or collusion, they soon get shamed by the audience."

Vince showed him a clip that demonstrated the whole system working, well enough. The question was ingenious, and the contestants struggled and failed. But when they raised a challenge, the questioners demonstrated an easy route to the answer, and in the end, no one argued with the adjudicators.

"This will take some coordination between the schools," Mr. Randall warned him. "And the students elsewhere might not be interested."

"Of course," Vince conceded. But he'd already poked the wasp's nest of parochial pride with an informal online challenge, and he was sure there'd soon be plans to join the competition underway in other schools.

It took eight weeks of organizing before the first round finally started. West Ryde was pitted against Denistone, with Zach, Wahid, and Mira joining Vince, while Leon had agreed to be an adjudicator at Eastwood versus Epping.

The event began half an hour after the last class on a Monday, and the audience easily fitted into a single row of seats in the echoing hall. But there was a video feed going out, both live and recorded, and as Vince and his teammates took their place on stage, he was hoping for hard questions and a close run, bringing some prestige to the competition itself, whoever won.

Everyone introduced themselves. Imani, Sam, Kyle, and Dorothy looked confident, and Denistone had bused in about as many supporters as had turned up for the local team.

Imani asked the first question. "Throw a pair of six-sided dice. Then draw two cards, without replacement, from a shuffled deck of fifty-two. With the cards valued one to thirteen, black cards positive and red cards negative, what is the chance that the total value of the dice evenly divides the total value of the cards?"

Vince's team had five minutes to respond and only pens and paper to help them. They'd agreed in advance to work independently; if they reached different answers, they could share notes and argue about each other's methods.

The best strategy, Vince decided, would be the one that made the most of the problem's symmetries . . . and beyond the simple symmetries that came from swapping suites, he realized that if he grouped the total values for the cards into pairs, using a simple rule, there were always 196 ways to reach one or other of the pair. There were *exactly* as many ways to draw a total that was either twenty-six or one as there were to get twenty-five or two, twenty-four or three, and so on. Surely there was a way to exploit that and capture all the possibilities in a single calculation?

But the dice refused to play dice; the *seventeen* ways a throw of the dice could divide a total of twenty-four for the cards bore no relationship to the *two* ways they could divide a total for the cards of three.

He'd wasted time on a mirage. He started racing through the twenty-seven totals individually, but he was barely halfway through when the buzzer rang. Wahid and Zach put down their pens, equally frustrated. But Mira handed Vince a sheet with her final result circled, and he read from it aloud:

"Six hundred and seventy-seven out of three thousand nine hundred and seventy-eight."

Imani smiled, and Vince assumed that was a bad sign, but their rival seemed genuinely delighted as she gave the verdict: "Correct!"

There was a two-minute break before the round continued. "We could have split the work in two for that one and finished twice as fast," Mira noted.

"Not into four?" Zach asked, half joking.

"Better to have two answers to check against each other," Mira replied.

Vince asked the first question directed at Denistone. "Given a twelve-sided regular polygon, if you wrote down the areas of every triangle whose vertices are three distinct vertices of the polygon, how many different values would there be?"

As their opponents set to work, huddling and whispering to each other to plan their strategy, Vince found himself willing them to succeed. Let them find the best way to share the load, and the slickest tricks to simplify the calculations. Though his ultimate goal was to goad the self-appointed Best and Brightest to swoop down and join the fray, he also wanted his fellow humans to shine along the way.

The buzzer sounded. Imani said, "There are twelve possible shapes for the triangles, if you treat mirror images as identical, which come from the ways you can write twelve as a sum of three positive integers. But two of those shapes, from $2 + 2 + 8$ and $1 + 4 + 7$, have identical areas. So there are only eleven different values in the list."

"Correct!" Vince confirmed. He'd set a trap, and Denistone had found it and disarmed it . . . but that was much more gratifying than if they'd fallen right in.

It was Sam's turn to put a question to West Ryde. "Can you find an integer," he asked, "whose reciprocal has a recurring decimal with ten repeating digits, all of them different?"

Vince's first response was to silently scoff that *recurring decimals* were primary school mathematics, so the problem ought to take thirty seconds at most. But then he realized he had no idea at all how to solve it efficiently.

Wahid said, "One-seventh is 0.142857 recurring, because seven times 142,857 is 999,999. Don't we just need something similar, with ten nines instead of six?"

Mira winced. "Yeah . . . we just need to factor a ten-digit number by hand."

"Three divides it once, then again," Zach volunteered. "Then eleven." But once those factors had been taken out, they were left with 101,010,101, which no longer yielded new divisors at a glance.

They started testing other small primes, splitting up the sequence between the four of them. Vince had just ruled out thirteen and twenty-nine when Wahid declared that forty-one was a bull's-eye, leaving them with 2,463,661.

"Is this the point where we build our own quantum computer out of sticks and bottle caps?" Zach asked plaintively.

Mira said, "Hang on. There's one obvious number that divides the thing with ten nines: the thing with five ones."

"Which is not divisible by eleven," Vince noted, "but . . . is it divisible by forty-one?"

It was: 11,111 divided by 41 gave 271, which Vince knew was prime. Zach divided their daunting partial result, 2,463,661, by 271, bringing it down to 9,091.

Mira said, "That smells like a prime to me . . . but I don't think we have time to check."

Vince looked to the clock; they only had ninety seconds left to make sense of these fragments. Multiplying all the definitely prime factors they'd found gave them 1,099,989, which didn't have enough digits, let alone distinct ones. They could start throwing in 9,091 and leave out some other factors, but . . . which ones, exactly?

"If the answer is big, the reciprocal could have three or four zeroes at the start before it begins repeating," Wahid realized. "So we really should be looking for factors of numbers with ten nines followed by a few zeroes."

Vince stared at the seven-digit number they'd reached. "Try multiplying this by 125," he told Wahid. "I'll try 128." Powers of two or five, divisors of the extra factors of ten.

Vince started calculating, but halfway through, he'd already produced nine twice. Then Wahid slid a sheet across the table, with his own result: he'd multiplied by a thousand then divided by eight, yielding 137,498,625. Every digit exactly once—including an unwritten zero at the start, which in the fraction would become visible, and also be repeated.

The buzzer rang. Vince gestured to Wahid to do the honors.

"We factored the number with ten nines and three zeroes," Wahid explained, "into 137,498,625 and 9,091 times eight, which is . . . 72,728. So the reciprocal of 72,728 has all ten digits repeating."

"That's correct," Sam conceded.

The audience cheered, and some of the meager home crowd stomped on the wooden floor. Vince was elated, but also exhausted and amazed; he felt like the four of them had just sprinted up a hill backward, shouting advice and encouragement to each other along the way.

Wahid had the next question for Denistone. "In the jellybean factory, six chutes emerge into the packing room, arranged in a circle. Going clockwise around the circle, they supply red only, green only, blue only, mixed green and blue, mixed red and blue, and mixed red and green jellybeans. But all the labels for the chutes have fallen off, so although you know the sequence of colors, you don't know where it starts. If you can sample at most one jellybean from each chute, what is the average number of jellybeans required to be sure you know exactly what every chute supplies?"

When the buzzer rang, Kyle announced confidently, "You always need at least two samples, but never more than four. On average, it takes two and five-eighths. But what happens to the black jellybeans?"

"They get diverted to my private supply," Wahid replied. "But your answer is correct."

After the break, Kyle rose to his feet again. "The Acme bus company runs services for one intercity route every three days, for another route every five days, and for a third route every six days. Their competitor, Zoetrope, wants to service the same three routes, with the same kind of regular timing, no less often than weekly, but they never want buses running the same route on the same day as their competitor. How many possible schedules does Zoetrope have to choose from?"

Vince wrote down the crucial numbers: three, five, six. The simplest way to avoid a clash would be to match Acme's frequencies on each route, while choosing a different offset for the days. But for the third route, Zoetrope could also avoid clashes by running buses every second or third day.

That gave him a total of $2 \times 4 \times (5 + 1 + 2) = 64$. But when he looked around to see if any of his teammates had finished their own calculations, he saw that Mira had arrived at $(2 + 4) \times 4 \times (5 + 1 + 2) = 192$.

"Where does the extra four come from, for the first route?" Vince asked. As he was speaking, Wahid handed him a sheet with 192 as the result, then Zach said, "I get sixty-four."

Mira said, "The first route can run every three days, in one of two slots, but also *every six days*, in any of four slots."

"Ah, of course." Vince turned to Zach, who said, "Okay, I get it. But you can't pull the same trick on the other routes, because doubling the gap would make it less than weekly."

The buzzer rang, and Mira rose to tender their result. But Kyle said, "I'm sorry, that's not correct. There are ten choices for the third route."

"Why?" Mira demanded. "The gap needs to divide six, and then there are one fewer slots than the gap. The divisors are six, three, and two, so the slot counts are five, two, and one."

"The gaps don't need to divide six," Kyle replied. "A gap of four days would work just as well, starting either one day after one of the Acme buses, or three days after."

Mira thought it over. "You're right." She nodded resignedly and took her seat.

"How did we miss that?" she asked her teammates.

Zach said, "The same way Vince and I missed the case you caught. We all thought the pattern was simpler than it was."

A chime marked the end of the break, and Mira rose to ask her own question.

She said, "People are standing in a queue, waiting to get into a concert. The promoters decide to give away some free merch, using the following system. Every ticket to the concert includes a twenty-digit random number; the promoters obtain their own random number from a spare ticket they're holding, then everyone in the queue checks whether their number is higher or lower than that. Starting from the second place in the queue, every second person receives a free T-shirt if they fall into the same group—'higher' or 'lower'—as the majority of people ahead of them. As the queue grows longer, what is the probability that a new person joining in an even-numbered position will receive a free T-shirt?"

Vince watched the opposition as they absorbed the question; some of them were smiling as if they'd cracked the whole thing already. He tried to regain his original spirit of generosity toward them, but it was a struggle to cheer them on now that West Ryde's place in the competition was at risk.

The buzzer sounded, and Dorothy announced her team's consensus. "One half," she said. "That's the limit as the queue gets longer."

"That's not correct," Mira replied. "The answer is three-quarters."

Dorothy was silent for a moment, but she didn't seem entirely surprised. "We'd like to see a derivation," she said.

Mira walked over to the whiteboard and picked up a blue marker. Starting from the fact that all the ticket-holders, including the promoters, were equally likely to appear in every possible order when ranked according to the tickets' random numbers, it only took a few lines of algebra to show that the probability for the nth person in the queue to get a T-shirt, when n was even, was $(3n + 2) / (4n + 4)$. As n grew larger, this approached three-quarters.

"So that's a draw!" the chief adjudicator proclaimed, addressing the camera. "Congratulations to both teams. Thanks for watching, and don't forget to check out the other two matches that were in play this afternoon."

The rivals came together and shook hands. "We just got lost with that last one," Vince heard Imani confess to Mira. "We convinced ourselves it was a half, by symmetry."

As he walked home, slowly—his body inexplicably aching, as if he'd just been through some kind of physical ordeal—Vince mulled over the failures he'd witnessed. It was easy to get trapped by the sense that you'd grasped the essence of a problem, then let that steer the calculations. His own team hadn't made any arithmetical errors in the bus scheduling problem, they'd just stopped looking for solutions beyond the obvious ones. And he was entirely sympathetic to the lure of symmetry that had mesmerized Denistone.

And the Cyranos? What would mesmerize them, or hide in their own blind spots?

After dinner, Vince sat in his room and watched the other matches. Epping had defeated Eastwood, three to two, and Dundas and Meadowbank had drawn, two all. There were some tough questions, and he would need to go over the videos with his team at their next training session. But for now, he just let the scents of the three problems he'd grappled with resonate in his brain, as he lay down and closed his eyes and waited for the gargoyle to do its thing.

7

In the second round of the competition, West Ryde defeated Dundas, three points to two. In the third round, they did the same to Meadowbank. In the fourth, they tied with Epping, two all, and in the fifth, they tied with Eastwood, three all.

Epping emerged from the five rounds with fourteen points, West Ryde with thirteen, Eastwood with eleven, and the other three teams with ten.

"This is exciting!" Vince's father said over dinner when he learned that they'd made it to the final. "The whole family will be there to cheer you on."

"No, you should just stream it," Vince urged him.

"We won't embarrass you," his mother promised. "We're not going to wave a big banner and shout your name."

"We *will* shout your name," Ethan interjected.

"I won't," Carol said, glaring at Ethan.

Vince said, "It's just . . . it'll be easier to concentrate if I'm not thinking about anything else."

His father said, "All right. I get it. We can watch from home."

They continued the meal in silence; no one else seemed to have any news to share. His father had completed his refrigeration certificate, but so far, he'd been unable to get a single interview. His mother had been doing volunteer work in a charity shop for the last eighteen months, but now she'd been told that the shop was closing down.

"Whoever wins the final," Vince said, "I'm hoping that won't be the end of it. I'm hoping they'll widen the competition and bring in a few more schools."

His father smiled. "Not content with conquering the northern suburbs? You want to be national champions?"

Vince said, "I wouldn't go that far. I'd be happy with just one more match."

Epping had never lost, though, and even if West Ryde held them to another draw, Epping would win on points. For his team to be the ones to take on their real adversaries, they'd still need an unprecedented victory first.

8

Wahid put the first question to Epping. "Give a polynomial in x and y with integer coefficients whose zero set looks like two decimal digits with the same height and width, and where the two-digit number they represent is the coefficient of x in each of the polynomial's factors."

Hardeep, Gemma, Lance, and Eunice spent about thirty seconds discussing strategy before setting to work. Vince was in two minds about the difficulty of their task; the number portrayed could really only be eighty or eighty-eight. Still, typesetting digits as algebraic curves required a certain attention to detail, and under pressure, anyone could make a mistake.

"Can we just write the answer, rather than reading it out loud?" Hardeep asked the chief adjudicator, Thomas.

"Go ahead," Thomas replied.

The three factors Hardeep wrote on the whiteboard were exactly the ones Wahid had chosen: an eight formed from two circular loops, and a zero from an adjacent ellipse.

Hardeep's question for West Ryde toyed with the infinite. "A merry-go-round with a radius of eight meters rotates twice every minute. Halfway out from the center sits a one-eighth scale replica of the entire merry-go-round, rotating at the same rate, which includes a replica of the replica, and so on. There are eight horses on the merry-go-round, arranged evenly around the perimeter, and the center of the first replica lines up with one of the horses. If each full-scale horse weighs fifty kilograms, what is the total momentum of all the horses at a moment when the centers of all the merry-go-rounds line up on one straight line?"

Vince believed he could see a clear path ahead, and it seemed safer to talk it through with his teammates than have them all work separately and compare notes at the end. "All the top-level horses' momenta add up to zero," he said, "by symmetry. And for each of the lower levels, it's almost as good: their velocities add up to the number of horses times the velocity of their own merry-go-round's center." From there, all the scaling and summing was easy enough, in principle, but complicated enough for errors to slip in.

Zach, Wahid, and Mira checked his algebra, and then they all tackled the arithmetic of plugging in the specific numerical values. They reached a consensus a few seconds before the buzzer.

Vince said, "The total momentum to four decimal places is 0.6561 kilogram-meters per second. But I can write out the exact fraction of pi if you prefer."

Hardeep said, "That's correct. No need for the precise value."

Vince delivered the next question to Epping. "A special coin has been minted in the shape of a regular twelve-sided polygon. Each side is eight millimeters long, and the coin is two millimeters thick. Imagine tossing it into the air, then taking a snapshot, freezing it in mid-flight at a random moment. Repeat this, over and over again. If every possible way the coin could be oriented in these snapshots is equally likely, what's the average difference in height between the highest and lowest points on the coin?"

He watched his rivals as they absorbed the scenario, extracting the geometric essence of the problem. Then he waited, tensed, half expecting them to respond in a minute or two; if they did, he'd have no one but himself to blame. But he still felt better about asking a question where the answer became insanely easy if you found the right approach, than one where you had to slog through endless computations regardless.

The buzzer rang. Gemma wrote Epping's result on the whiteboard in fractions and square roots, adding, "It comes to about fifteen and a half."

Vince said, "That's not correct. The average is exactly twenty-five millimeters."

Gemma laughed curtly. "That can't be right! We might be off slightly, but we must be close. The coin's longest diagonal is about thirty-one millimeters. When you take the average height of a line segment over all orientations, you get half its length. So it has to be close to fifteen and a half."

"Do you want me to give my derivation?" Vince asked.

"Go ahead."

He joined her at the whiteboard. "You can generate the shape of this coin by taking seven line segments," he began. "Six that correspond to consecutive edges of one face of the coin, and one that corresponds to an edge that's perpendicular to both faces. If you add up every possible choice of seven points from those seven line segments—treating each point as a vector—you get a twelve-sided prism that matches the shape of the coin."

Vince drew a sketch showing how the first six segments created a single polygonal face, which was then extruded into a prism by adding points from the seventh segment.

After staring at the diagram for a while, Gemma said, "Okay, I think I agree with you so far. But what does that prove?"

Vince said, "Adding up the points from these segments, then projecting them onto a vertical line is the same as projecting them first and then adding them up. So we can get the projection of *the entire coin* that way. But we know that the average height of each projection is half the length of the original segment—just as you said—so the average of the sum of those heights is half the sum of the segments' lengths: six times eight plus two gives fifty, halved gives twenty-five. So the average vertical distance, from the lowest point in the coin to the highest, is twenty-five millimeters."

Gemma walked back to the table and conferred with her team. "You're right," she said. "We concede."

There was some applause from the audience, but even West Ryde's most enthusiastic supporters sounded more cautious than triumphalist. Their team still couldn't afford to get a single question wrong.

"An ornamental fish vendor has twenty rare fish on sale, for a hundred dollars each," Gemma began. "The weight of any given fish has a fifty percent chance of being three grams, a twenty-five percent chance of being two grams, and a twenty-five percent chance of being four grams. Unbeknownst to the vendor, you're certain that one of these fish has swallowed a diamond ring, worth a thousand dollars and weighing five grams. If you buy some of the fish, you could identify one with the ring by weighing them all individually, but you could only resell the others at half price. The vendor will let you use their scales just once to weigh any single group of fish you like, before you choose the ones you purchase. What should you do to maximize your expected profit?"

Vince was tempted to reply: *buy the fish that's struggling the hardest to retain its buoyancy.*

"So we weigh some number of fish," Mira suggested, "then either buy them, or buy all the others, depending on the result?"

"I can't think of any other strategy," Wahid replied, and neither could Vince or Zach.

Vince stared at the notes he'd made on the possible weights for a single fish—two, three, or four grams—with their associated probabilities of a quarter, a half, and a quarter. What they needed was the same kind of table for a batch of any number of fish . . . but with three different weights involved, surely that was going to be some kind of trinomial nightmare?

Then he realized that the shortcut Epping had built into the problem was hiding in plain sight. "Those 'quarter, half, quarter' probabilities are exactly the same as you get for the head counts from tossing a fair coin twice," he said. "So if we weigh f fish, the weights will just follow the probabilities for tossing twice as many coins."

"But what's the best f?" Mira asked. "And the best threshold weight to buy on?" She thought for a while. "I bet it's close to half the total on sale, and the threshold weight is close to the mean."

Vince found her hunch persuasive, though he couldn't see how to make it exact or quantify the correction if it wasn't. "So we hunt around the middle," he proposed. "Weigh ten, nine, eight fish, and look at the payoff if we buy the batch when it's greater than or equal to three grams per fish."

Zach said, "I'd bump up the threshold for the total weight of the batch by at least three grams. Because the ring's five."

"Yes," Mira agreed.

They allocated a handful of cases between them, and it was soon clear that for a given number of fish, Zach's version of the threshold weight was exactly on target; raising or lowering it always gave a lower yield. But as they went from ten fish down to eight, the payoff was still rising: $324.99, $333.19, $334.40. *Had it peaked, or not?*

"What's seven?" Vince pleaded. But they only had thirty seconds remaining, and no one had even started the calculation.

The buzzer rang.

Vince exchanged glances with his teammates to see if anyone else wanted to make the call. But they didn't, so he rose to his feet.

"To maximize your expected profits, you should weigh eight of the fish," he declared. "If the weight is twenty-seven grams or more, buy those eight fish. Otherwise, buy the remaining twelve."

Gemma said, "Correct."

Vince sat down as the cheers broke out. An informed guess wasn't cheating; they weren't expected to supply a watertight proof. But he would have felt better if they'd managed to verify that the payoff for seven fish was lower.

Zach asked the last question for Epping. "Two spacecraft, piloted by a smuggler and a customs inspector, are a certain distance apart, and initially at rest with respect to each other. If the smuggler accelerates straight toward the inspector at the maximum rate its engines allow, never changing course, while the inspector's spacecraft accelerates at twice that rate, the inspector can match both the velocity and the position of the smuggler in exactly one hour. But if the inspector wanted to reduce the time from one hour to thirty minutes, what ratio would their spacecraft's acceleration need to have to the smuggler's?"

Vince felt sure now that the problem was too easy, but it was too late to fret about that. He tried to relax and prepare himself for whatever was coming next. He gulped down all the chilled water that remained in his flask; it sloshed around inside him, distending his stomach, but then the cooling sensation in his throat, and a sense of clarity that seemed to flow up through his palate, more than made up for the discomfort.

Lance said, "The ratio of accelerations needed to halve the interception time is three plus the square root of ten."

"That's correct," Zach acknowledged.

The applause from the local crowd was raucous and impassioned. Vince felt a surge of camaraderie, both for the team and for their supporters. He still desperately wanted to defeat them, but they were all celebrating the same human skills.

Lance stood to deliver the final question. "Take an isosceles triangle with a height five-eighths of its base and cut it into four pieces that can be reassembled as a square. Exactly one of the pieces is a right-angled triangle. What is the area of that triangle as a fraction of the whole?"

Wahid started making sketches. Since the original triangle had no right angles, the four corners of the square had to arise from the various cut lines meeting each other at ninety degrees. One possibility would be a single cut lopping the triangle into two pieces, which were then each divided by cuts perpendicular to the first one. If the main cut and one side cut both had endpoints on the same edge of the original triangle, that would produce the sole triangular piece; the other three pieces would be quadrilaterals.

"How do we make sure these bits all fit together?" Wahid asked.

"Match some angles to get rid of any kinks, and some lengths . . . ?" He rubbed his temples, agitated.

Vince wished he could leap in and provide a clear answer; the criteria ought not be all that complicated. But he couldn't keep the geometry straight in his head. They didn't have scissors to physically perform the dissection, so he redrew the pieces, recombined in a rough square. But as he struggled to identify which angles needed to do what in order to keep the square's sides straight, Zach began drawing a new version of his own.

"What if we extend each piece of the triangle into a separate copy of the square?" he said, illustrating the idea: every piece stayed where it was, but by adding adjoining copies of the other three pieces around it, four squares appeared, each one identically chopped into four.

Mira said, "Now do the same thing with the squares: grow each piece into a triangle of its own."

Zach complied; each square sprouted three more triangles, though there was some overlap between them. "And again," he said, filling in pieces to make more squares, and then more triangles.

The page was now covered in a mosaic, a periodic arrangement of the four pieces of the dissection that the eye could group together *either* as strips of adjoining squares or strips of triangles pointing alternately up and down.

It made the nature of the dissection obvious, but they still needed to quantify everything. The whole team worked on the geometric fine print and cross-checked the results, transforming Zach's sketch from an appeal to the eye into a watertight mathematical promise. Vince finally looked at the clock; forty seconds remained, and this time a guess would not be good enough. They had everything they needed to find the area of the triangular piece, but it was going to take a few more calculations.

As the buzzer rang, he was still writing out the last step. He put down his pen and looked up from the page, performing the final multiplication in his head.

"The square root of two and one-fifth," he said. "Divided by eight."

Lance said, "That's correct." He lowered his gaze for a moment, clearly fighting to overcome his disappointment, but then he faced his opponents and addressed them graciously. "Congratulations," he said. "You earned the win, and we'll look forward to a rematch next year."

9

"I need a favor," Vince told Jamie, after finally tracking him down with just minutes to spare before the start of fourth period.

Jamie regarded him with a mixture of amusement and mild surprise, but no hostility. They'd never been close friends, but Vince had always got on well with him, prior to his ascent into the cultural stratosphere. He knew he was being presumptuous, but it wasn't as if he were a former tormentor coming to beg forgiveness or trying to pretend that he'd always been on the victim's side.

"I'm not going to dance at anyone's party," Jamie replied. "Not for money, not for exposure."

"Exposure?"

"Some millionaire wanted me to perform for free at a fundraiser for the state opera, and the payoff was that all the beautiful people would be talking about me."

Vince said, "All I want is a shout-out for the AQ. I want to rub some faces in it."

"You mean . . . 'West Ryde triumphs over Epping! Woo-hoo!' Isn't that what the school mascot is for?"

"It's not like that," Vince replied. "I just want to get under the skin of the Cyrano users." And the faux-anime marsupial that announced all of West Ryde's sporting wins had a follower count in the low double digits.

Jamie seemed puzzled for a moment, then he grinned with delight. "You want to take them on? But you want them to be the ones to lay down the challenge? To think it's their own idea?"

"Yes."

"I'm always happy to talk up the humans," Jamie declared, "but I'm not sure that many Cyranos watch my channel." Jamie had invested some of his busking money in a camera that cryptographically signed its output, proving that the routines he recorded weren't fake, and last time Vince had checked, he had more than six million subscribers.

Vince said, "Every little bit helps."

That night, Jamie ad-libbed a few sentences about the Adversarial Quiz. Vince had contemplated trying to script something, but he was glad he hadn't; Jamie's own words sounded, if not utterly spontaneous, more like the product of his personal musings on intelligence and creativity than something he'd been pressed into service to deliver.

Over the next few days, Vince followed the subsequent chatter online. Only a tiny fraction of Jamie's viewers had anything to say on the subject, but the mere fact that they were endorsing his celebration of human prowess invited pushback, in part from people calling him a hypocrite because he'd got his own start via a machine. Then came the second wave, pointing out that Jamie's exo had only acquired the means to guide him at all by studying a million hours of footage of human dancers.

And as for the significance of unaided humans vying against each other at AQ . . . those who found it uplifting were soon in heated battle with those who considered it a joke. "One Cyrano would wipe the floor with those Neanderthals!" Symbiont621 opined. "In what universe would anyone need to solve a real problem without a bot beside them?" VibePilot4943 scoffed.

After a week or so, the whole topic fizzled out, but Vince didn't give up hope. What mattered, in the end, was not the level of ongoing bluster from full-time shitposters, but any lingering unease the discussion had provoked in the administrators of Cyrano-friendly schools, whose marketing strategy relied on assuring parents that their little darlings—rather than growing weak and over-reliant on their tech—would be permanently, and incontrovertibly, lofted high above the unaugmented riffraff.

A month after the AQ final, Vince received a message from Mr. Randall. "Trentham College has sent their congratulations to West Ryde's Adversarial Quiz team on their recent win. Also, their principal wants to invite the team to a demonstration match! What do you think? It sounds strange to me. You four with pens and paper, and the other team with built-in AIs. But talk it over with your friends, and let me know how you want to reply."

10

As the bus turned off the street into the entrance road, nothing about Trentham College struck Vince as being much different from any other upmarket private school. The buildings were sandstone, possibly predating electric light, and the sports fields were so vast and uniformly green that they looked less like genuine vegetation than something from a video game. He could see a group of students playing field hockey, so distant that their shouts were barely audible.

"That's a letdown," Mira said. "I was expecting a polo match at the very least."

"They must be waiting for approval to give the ponies their own chips," Wahid suggested.

"Is your cousins' school like this?" Vince asked Zach.

"The grounds are smaller," Zach replied.

"In proportion to the fees?" Mira joked.

"In proportion to the students' laziness. They'd never put up with having to walk that far."

When the bus had parked in a spot marked and reserved for them, West Ryde's team and supporters were greeted by three members of the Trentham Student Council who escorted them into the Great Hall. The present audience did not come close to filling the stained-glass cavern, but it still outnumbered any of the crowds Vince had seen at previous matches, including the final against Epping.

One of the Councilors introduced the team to the adjudicators—generously supplied by Epping, Eastwood, and Denistone—and their opposition, Matthew and Cybil. It was Trentham who'd proposed that a team of two AI-human pairs would be a suitable match for four humans, and Vince had seen no reason to oppose the composition. If anything, it undersold the claims by Hyperfine that a single pair would soon replace a dozen people, right across the knowledge-based workforce.

As Vince shook Cybil's hand, she met his gaze, and he felt a frisson of unease. He did not believe that Cyranos were conscious, but Cybil herself was still a different kind of person than he was accustomed to dealing with. What was it like to swim through life with an untiring companion, fluent and apparently endlessly knowledgeable, catching your mistakes, offering advice, feeding you *bons mots* and tips on etiquette as easily as it solved partial differential equations? His own tutors were crude and bumbling even when they managed to dollop out the curriculum without errors, but whatever the Cyranos' flaws in their attempts to grasp the complexity of the world, it was rare for their critics to fail to acknowledge their silver tongues.

The teams and the adjudicators took their seats, then Cybil rose, and the audience fell silent.

"In the wizard's castle in the Bavarian Forest," Cybil began, "the enchanted mice play a game with the grandfather clock. A minute or two before each hour strikes, they swarm out from their hiding place and take turns moving the hour hand around, making sure to return it to the correct position by the time the clock chimes.

"Each mouse has instructions to move the hand by first multiplying the angle measured clockwise from midnight by a certain factor, then advancing it by a certain number of hours. Both numbers must appear on the clockface, but the multiplier must satisfy a further requirement: if its *square* were used to multiply the angle, that would return the hand to its original position.

"Each mouse has their own unique pair of numbers, and between them they encompass all the possibilities the rules allow. But to keep them from growing bored, every month the wizard switches the numbers around. He picks a pair of mice whose instructions, if performed one after the other, would bring the clock's hour hand back to where it started. Call these mice 'Andersen' and 'Grimm.' Then, for each mouse, the wizard determines the overall effect of performing first Grimm's, then the mouse's, then Andersen's instructions—as they were for the previous month—and he gives these new numbers to the mouse for the month to follow.

"All of this worked splendidly for many years, but then the wizard's cousin came to visit while the change was taking place, and he asked why it was performed this way. The wizard replied that, though each mouse's instructions varied from month to month, any sequence of mice whose combined shenanigans returned the hour hand to where it had started would find that their actions continued to yield the same result, even after the change. No other system, the wizard suggested, could ensure that that remained the case.

"The cousin thought for a while, then told the wizard that there was another way. He offered a method with the same guarantee, but though it could be mimicked for each mouse individually by choosing their own personal 'Andersen' and 'Grimm,' it could never have followed from applying the wizard's old method, where just one pair of mice took on those roles for everyone.

"The question, then, is can you give a formula that the cousin might have used for this new way to change the mice's numbers?"

Vince's teammates looked as if they'd just been ambushed by a bad bedtime story, so he did his best to break the spell. "Strip away the flowery language, and the mice are just functions that take x to a times x plus b. Everything is done in modular arithmetic, with x and b ranging from zero to eleven. But a needs its square to be one, modulo twelve, so: one, five, seven, eleven. That means every mouse function has an inverse, and the inverse of a times x plus b is just a times x minus a times b."

Mira said, "Cool." Almost deadpan, but with the faintest hint of trepidation. Trentham had chosen to evoke West Ryde's first error, the bus scheduling problem, which had also involved modular arithmetic. But surely they knew that their opponents would have worked hard to address that weakness? So . . . perhaps they were counting on a sense of complacency, now that the hole had supposedly been so thoroughly patched?

But Vince didn't have time to ponder these mind games. "Okay, what's the wizard's usual method for altering the mouse functions? That's just conjugation: you sandwich one function between another one and its inverse—the 'Andersen' and the 'Grimm.'"

Wahid had an "aha!" moment. "And if a whole string of different functions canceled out before the change, then *after* the change, the Andersens and Grimms you wrapped around them will also cancel out, and the clock hand will still end up back where it started."

"So the wizard's method works," Zach said, "but what the hell is the cousin up to?"

Vince said, "The cousin's formula always has to look like the result of *some* conjugation." He wrote:

If $f(x) = a x + b$ and $g(x) = c x + d$
conjugation is $g(f(g^{-1}(x))) = a x + (b c + d (1 - a))$

"Except the cousin gets to choose a different c and d for each mouse," Mira noted. "For forty-eight mice, that's some astronomical number of options."

"What if we fix c, and make d depend on a alone?" Vince suggested. "And for a consistency check . . . " He worked through the effects of one mouse with an a of seven followed by another with an a of five, before and after the cousin's change, and ended up with the formula:

$Z(11) = Z(5) + 5 Z(7)$
where $Z(a) = d(a) (1 - a)$

Mira started listing the choices for Z, for the three a values that mattered: five, seven, and eleven. There were only six possibilities:

0, 0, 0
8, 6, 2
4, 0, 4
0, 6, 6

8, 0, 8
4, 6, 10

Wahid said, "Each of these has the same *d* for all the *a*s. They're just
d from zero to five!"

Vince could see that now. "Okay. So where did we go wrong?"

No one answered him, but they all began rechecking everything
in sight. Then Zach emitted a sudden groan. "The castle's in frigging
Bavaria. Germany uses *twenty-four-hour time*."

Vince looked to the adjudicators' un-Bavarian clock; the team had
slightly more than a minute to recover from the misstep.

He took the simplest of Mira's examples, 0, 6, 6, and began to reinterpret
it. Modulo twenty-four, the first six was *three* times one minus seven,
while the second six was . . . *nine* times one minus eleven, so different *d*s,
different Andersens and Grimms. They were in the clear.

Now they just had to find the next four numbers, for *a* of thirteen,
seventeen, nineteen, and twenty-three. Vince guessed they could set *Z* of
thirteen equal to zero, then get the rest by generalizing the consistency
formula, replacing the five and seven with other values.

When the buzzer rang, he stood and spoke calmly, though his legs
were trembling. "One method the cousin could have used would be to
multiply by . . . "—Vince realized he hadn't made a choice for *c*, so he
grabbed one from thin air—" . . . five the number of hours each mouse
advanced the clock's hand, then add six if their angle factor was equal to
seven, eleven, nineteen, or twenty-three . . . with all of this arithmetic
performed modulo twenty-four."

Cybil said, "Correct."

The cheers and shouts from the West Ryde supporters drowned out
the polite applause from the Cyrano pairs. Vince's spirits soared, even
as he imagined the online commentary: *hamstrung by rules limiting
their questions to those an unaided human could handle, the Cyranos
never had a chance to display their true, superhuman skills.* But the real
test would come when the roles were reversed; no one was throttling
the Cyranos' power to find answers.

"Every Sunday for the past thirty years," Zach began, "Peter has gone
for a sixteen-kilometer hike along the same route near his home. But
last weekend, he and his wife were visiting her parents, so he went for
a hike of about the same length along a different route.

"Every time he hikes, Peter records any sightings of four animals
that are common in the region: the yellow and brown lemmings and
the gray and white skinks. The yellow lemmings and the gray skinks

are only seen at altitudes below one hundred meters, while the brown lemmings and the white skinks are only seen above four hundred meters.

"If the sightings for each animal are grouped by which quarter of the hike they were made in, they form a four-by-four square." Zach proceeded to list, not the contents of each square, but the row sums, the column sums, and the sums along seven diagonals, for the sightings made on Peter's most recent hike near his own home, and the hike near his parents-in-law's house.

"On Monday morning, Peter's wife asked him what the biggest difference was between the hikes in the two places. His reply contained a six-letter word in English that can describe certain kinds of animals. What was that word most likely to be?"

The information provided was not enough to reconstruct all the data, but it did constrain it. Vince expected the Cyranos to have enumerated the possibilities in a fraction of a second—but what came next would depend on exactly how the results were analyzed and shared with the humans.

The buzzer sounded, and Cybil rose to present her team's response. "Given that lemmings are a kind of *rodent* and skinks are a kind of *lizard*, those are two obvious candidates for the answer. Peter might also have used the word *alpine* to distinguish highland species from their lowland cousins. But the total numbers in each of these categories didn't differ strikingly between the two occasions. Using 'lizard' in lieu of 'skink' would be the least odd choice of phrasing—who would say 'rodent' when they meant 'lemming'?—but the variation in the skink numbers hardly seemed worth mentioning.

"That suggests that the data needs to be interpreted with a slightly different purpose in mind. We found that it was highly likely that Peter crossed between lowland and highland regions in *all four quarters* of his latest hike but only made *two* such crossings during the previous hike. That in turn makes it likely that the trail was considerably steeper for the second hike.

"So our answer is 'calves.' When his wife asked about the hike the next morning, Peter told her how much his calves were aching, since although he was used to long walks like this, he'd spent the last thirty years growing accustomed to a gentler slope."

"That's correct," Zach replied.

The applause from the Trentham supporters was decorous but emphatic, rising up in near-perfect synchrony, deafening for a moment, then falling away. Zach appeared crestfallen; his hope had been that the unembodied Cyranos wouldn't make the connection between the altitudes implied by the sightings and the effects of the hike on an actual human body—and they'd have no reason to mire their partners in unnecessary detail by mentioning anything but the animal numbers. But it appeared the collaboration was tighter than that, and even if the Cyranos hadn't thought of aching calves all by themselves, the humans—who'd more easily form a visceral image of a hiker struggling up a rocky trail—had not been limited to an executive summary with a two-dimensional map of the fauna's population counts.

Matthew put the next question to West Ryde.

"Start with a list of every possible eight-bit byte, from zero to two hundred and fifty-five. Suppose you transform all the bytes in this list by the following method: you choose eight bytes to use as masks, one for each bit of the new byte, and you set that bit to one or zero depending on whether an *odd* or *even* number of bits in the original byte are equal to one in places where the mask is also one.

"Depending on which masks you choose, this process might turn the original list into one where some of the bytes are missing and others are repeated. The question is, how many different ways can you choose the masks so that the new list is simply a reordering of the original, with nothing duplicated or omitted?"

Everyone on the team looked to each other. "Maybe do it for two bits, then three bits, and see if we can find a pattern?" Wahid proposed.

"Yes," Mira concurred. "For two bits, there are four different bytes . . . but picking 00 for a mask would be crazy, because it could never give you a one in that position. So you have three bytes to choose from for each mask." She quickly wrote out all nine possibilities and tested them on the list of four bytes. "Ah," she realized, "you can't use the same mask more than once because that forces all the new bytes to have *identical bits* in two places, which means the new list can never be complete."

Wahid said, "So for two bits there are six choices: three for the first mask, then two for the second. And for three bits there ought to be . . . seven times six times five, two hundred and ten."

"Hang on," Vince interjected. "I think that's just an upper limit. We know that repeating a mask would be bad, but it might not be the only way things can go wrong."

"What else can happen?" Wahid asked, unconvinced but willing to be persuaded.

Vince wasn't sure, but he couldn't believe the problem could be so simple. He said, "All this talk about bit masks is hiding something. There ought to be a clearer way to think about it."

"Like what?" Zach pressed him. "Because it feels like we're stumbling around inside a computer in the dark."

"I don't know." Vince glanced at the clock; they had a little more than three minutes remaining. "If the answer is just keeping the masks different, then there's no more work to do, but we need to check if it holds for three bits."

Wahid laughed. "You want us to check 210 sets of masks?"

"No," Vince conceded. "Let me think. What if there's a bit that isn't one for *any* of the masks? Say we had 010, 100, 110; that's three different masks, but the last bit is always zero. That will turn the byte 001 to 000, but 000 also gets transformed into 000, so now it's duplicated."

"Okay." Wahid was dismayed, but then he rallied. "So there's a stronger condition: for each position, *at least one mask* needs to have a one there. We can still account for that, can't we?"

Mira said, "Wait. If we can't have all zeroes in any bit position, maybe we can't have repetitions either—the same pattern across all masks in two different places? What happens with a four-bit mask set like . . . "

She wrote:

1 1 0 0
1 1 0 1
0 0 1 0
1 1 1 1

"These are all different masks," she said, "and there's no position that's always zero. But because we have 1101 across the masks for both of the first two bits, this turns 1100 into 0000."

"There's a kind of symmetry there," Wahid said hopefully.

"Between the rows and columns of a matrix," Vince realized belatedly. "All this crap about bit masks is just a way of talking about matrices."

"So where does that get us?" Zach asked.

Vince said, "We need to count all the eight-by-eight matrices whose entries are zero or one, and whose rows and columns aren't 'degenerate' . . . like two vectors that are parallel, or three vectors that lie in the same plane, because that wastes the chance to span one more dimension. But we need to do this in a space where the only coordinates are zero and one, and all arithmetic is modulo two."

Wahid wasn't giving up. "For three bits, what if we say . . . there are seven choices for the first row because we're avoiding zero; six choices for the second row because we're avoiding zero and the first row; and then *four* choices for the third row because we're avoiding zero, and the first two rows, *and* the vector you get by adding the first two rows together because the sum of two vectors lies in the same plane. Seven times six times four is 168. Does that make sense?"

The buzzer rang.

Vince stood up. "I'm sorry," he said. "We have no answer."

Matthew walked over to the whiteboard and wrote:

$$(28 - 20) \times (28 - 21) \times (28 - 22) \times (28 - 23) \times (28 - 24) \times (28 - 25) \times (28 - 26) \times (28 - 27) = 5{,}348{,}063{,}769{,}211{,}699{,}200$$

Vince didn't ask for an explanation; Matthew's answer just extended the pattern in Wahid's result for three bits: $(23 - 20) \times (23 - 21) \times (23 - 22) = 168$. For each row, you needed to exclude the sum of any selection from the previous rows—including single rows, or none at all—and there were two to the power of the row count such selections. They might have got there with a little more time.

In the break, they debated whether they should rethink their strategy against Trentham. They'd come prepared with ten questions, ready to make new choices from the list if necessary, and the failure of Zach's approach cast some of the rankings in a new light.

But the three original selections still targeted different potential weak spots. "I say we don't blink," Mira declared, and in the end, everyone agreed.

Mira rose to her feet. "A few years before the fall of the Berlin Wall," she said, "an English journalist was imprisoned in East Germany. She was able to exchange letters with her husband, but they knew their mail was being read by authorities. Among the first things her husband sent her was a computer printout of a poem, written by their twelve-year-old daughter, which the journalist kept pinned to the wall of her prison cell. It read:

"Evening light fades / Quiet descends / The joking boy relaxed / Sweetly amazed / Night promises peaceful dreams / Until morning.

"Historians studying the correspondence between the couple found that the words of this poem showed up in their letters far more often than would have been expected, and so might have played a part in a code they used.

"Once, in response to a letter where her husband used 'joking,' 'descends,' 'quiet,' 'fades,' and 'light,' in that order, the journalist responded by using 'evening,' 'amazed,' 'boy' three times, 'amazed,' 'evening,' 'joking' twice, 'relaxed,' 'sweetly,' 'amazed,' 'sweetly,' then 'relaxed.'

"What was she communicating?"

Cybil and Matthew received the question with an air of perfect equanimity. Vince averted his gaze to avoid the temptation to stare at them and try to guess the kind of dialogue they were having with their Cyranos.

"No one could miss that the poem is a pangram," Mira said quietly.

"You'd think not," Vince replied.

"But then the question is . . . " Zach began, before Mira put a finger to her lips.

When the buzzer rang, Matthew stood, frowning slightly. "The problem is severely under-determined," he declared. "There are literally thousands of algorithms that would map both the husband's code words and the journalist's to English plaintext, using the daughter's poem as a shared resource. The algorithm with the lowest complexity yields 'nine' from the husband and 'egg lignin' from the journalist. There are also protocols with more plausible exchanges, the simplest being 'cold' with the reply 'not very,' but the computational power required to implement them might have been prohibitive, especially for the journalist."

He waited, politely, for a response. Vince heard someone clear their throat out in the hall.

Mira rose to her feet. "The husband wasn't *saying* anything in his letter," she explained. "He was providing a key that the journalist could use to help encode her own message. She took his numbers—five, four, three, two, one, by their position in the poem, with 'evening' as zero and 'the' omitted—then used the dot matrix printout of the poem, with each letter of the alphabet forming a grid five dots wide, to transform them into a number for each row, adding up those with a matching dot, leaving out the rest. The lowercase letters 'o' and 'k' provided her response. She was saying 'okay.'"

Matthew turned to the adjudicators. "With respect, could anyone really have guessed that? The question didn't even mention a dot matrix printer."

Mira said, "What do you think home computers used in the nineteen-eighties? The question mentioned a computer printout—not typed, not handwritten."

The adjudicators conferred. Vince looked up at the vaulted ceiling. *Had the question been fair?* He believed so. And he certainly believed that an unaugmented human would have put themselves squarely in the shoes of the journalist from the start, thinking laterally about all the different ways the poem could be used, rather than getting sidetracked by the search for ever more elaborate and impractical algorithms that fit their initial preconceptions.

The chief adjudicator said, "We rule that no point be awarded, by a two-to-one decision."

The West Ryde supporters went wild, while the rest of the hall remained silent. Mira beamed at her teammates ecstatically. Vince felt lightheaded; the floor seemed to be endlessly tilting, trying to sweep the team offstage but never quite succeeding.

"The score is one all," the chief adjudicator declared, before inviting Trentham to continue.

Cybil rose to ask the second to last question of the match. "A goldsmith is given a cube of solid gold. They are told to think of it as comprising twenty-seven smaller cubic pieces and to remove seven of them: the one in the center of the cube, and the one in the center of each of its six faces. They are instructed to repeat this process for the remaining twenty smaller cubes, and so on . . . until an ice cube the size of the original cube, with this pared-down golden object frozen into it, would be light enough to float in water.

"Assume that the specific gravity of gold is exactly 19.28, and that of ice is 0.9168. Assume that the cube is large enough that the discrete, atomic nature of matter does not come into play.

"But now suppose that, rather than dividing each cube precisely into equal thirds along each axis, the fractions used are f, then f again, then one minus two f.

"The question is, by how much can f differ from one-third, while ensuring that the top of the floating cube, in equilibrium in still water, slopes by no more than one-hundredth of a degree?"

Vince felt as if he'd been smacked in the face with a cushion that had turned out to be a sandbag, which in turn had a lump of concrete at its core. Merely finding the point where the gold-inlaid ice cube would float would have been the softest of questions. Allowing this famous fractal construction—the Menger sponge—to be lopsided rendered everything far messier, though maybe not intractable. But having to solve a hydrostatic torque problem on top of that, in order to quantify the actual lopsidedness . . .

Mira said, "Eighteen iterations until it floats, if f is exactly one-third. But the specific gravity is about 0.9996, so we'll need to be careful."

Vince shook himself out of his stupor and wrote down the version of the density formula where f was allowed to change. A tiny drop below one-third would see the eighteenth iteration of the cube sink—a further evil twist to the problem that he was in no mood to admire.

Meanwhile, Wahid had been sketching waterlines. "These are the three ways the cube could break the surface of the water, if one corner has the most weight," he said. The cross section could be triangular, pentagonal, or rhombic, depending on the tilt and how much of the cube was submerged. "I'm guessing we'll need the volume and center of mass of the displaced water for each case."

Zach said, "Good idea. I'll shadow you."

Vince left them to it and turned to Mira. "We'll do the center of mass for the cube itself?"

She nodded, smiling slightly—maybe as terrified as he was by the moment of judgment barreling toward them, but determined to enjoy every remaining second nonetheless. "First, the gold alone, then add in the ice and combine them at the end?" she suggested.

"Yes!" That way, the densities wouldn't appear at all until the last minute, letting them focus on the geometry.

The center of mass of any rectangular block that appeared in the problem—even one with pieces removed in this lopsided fashion—should always lie on its main diagonal, running between the heaviest corner and the lightest. And at each level in the construction, the proportional distance along the diagonal to the center of mass should be the same for every block. So it ought to be possible to keep track of that single number, c, starting from one half for the tiniest blocks of solid gold, as they were assembled into ever more byzantine fractal agglomerations.

Vince added up the contributions from twenty suitably positioned blocks, then stared at the result, dismayed. The new value for c was a linear expression in the old c, but the coefficients were ratios between cubic and quadratic polynomials in f. Since f was still an unknown that needed to wend its way through all the subsequent calculations before its value could be found, applying this formula *eighteen times* would render the whole exercise impossibly unwieldy.

Mira examined what he'd written. "I get the same," she said.

"I was hoping I'd screwed up, and the real result was simpler," Vince confessed.

"This can't be as bad as it looks," Mira insisted. "There has to be a shortcut a human can perform with pen and paper, or they'd be afraid the adjudicators would rule against them."

"We could use an approximation that holds when f is close to one-third," Vince suggested tentatively.

"But we'd still have to iterate it eighteen times, right?" Mira glanced at the clock. Vince didn't follow her gaze, but he knew they had no hope of doing anything eighteen times.

"And then, does it blow up, or does it narrow down?" Mira wondered. "Because if it narrows . . . "

Vince felt a surge of adrenaline, as if she'd just yanked him back from the edge of a pit. "It must have a *fixed point*," he realized. For any f, there had to be a value of c that their updating formula left unchanged—and wherever they started from, each iteration ought to bring them closer to it.

He solved for the fixed point. They'd just have to hope that after eighteen iterations the gap between this and the real value was too small to matter.

Zach and Wahid had been looking on, waiting to report. Wahid said, "The bad news is, the cases where the top of the cube is partly underwater are horrendous. For such a small tilt, we might not need them . . . but if the whole thing's close to sinking, it's hard to be sure."

Vince said, "Okay. Let's see how far we get with the simplest case."

As f was increased above one-third, the cube became less dense and rose slightly higher in the water even as it tilted. It hit the designated angle with the top of the cube still entirely above the waterline.

But if you reduced f?

The buzzer rang with the question unresolved, so Vince stood and offered what they had. "The fraction f can increase by about 0.00028 before the cube tips by one-hundredth of a degree. But we didn't have time to determine what happens when it decreases."

Cybil said, "Your answer is correct, as far as it goes. The amount by which f can decrease is about half as much."

The adjudicators discussed the result among themselves, then the chief adjudicator announced, "We've agreed, unanimously, to award half a point to West Ryde."

Vince took his seat, dazed, trying to make sense of the strange reprieve. A win was still possible, and so was a loss; everything would be decided by the final question.

"What do we ask now?" he wondered.

"Stick to the plan," Zach counseled. They'd targeted awareness of the body and failed; they'd targeted empathy and succeeded. But having shown their hand, there was no point trying to repeat that victory.

The break ended, and Vince rose to speak again.

"You can take any ordinary sentence in English," he said, "and interpret it as a number by stripping out all spaces and punctuation, converting all letters to upper case, and treating the decimal digits zero to nine and the letters A to Z as digits in base thirty-six. For example, 'To be, or not to be' becomes a thirteen-digit number in base thirty-six.

"Now, consider a piece of text that manages to describe exactly the same number as its own base thirty-six interpretation. Its intended audience is someone who reads English and who knows all the details of the method I just gave to convert text into a number. But there are some restrictions. The text can't talk directly about itself; it can't just say, 'Interpret this sentence as base thirty-six.' It can't be a single decimal digit, which would make the problem trivial—or something like 007, for the same reason. And though it can be terse and blunt, it can't use emojis or textese, it can't omit spaces between words, and it can't assume that the reader will recognize and follow instructions in some programming language.

"What's the shortest string of characters—including spaces and punctuation marks—that satisfies all of these requirements?"

As Vince resumed his seat, Matthew and Cybil remained poker-faced. The problem he'd posed was related to "quines," computer programs whose output matched their own source code, but were forbidden to cheat by simply printing their own file. Some recreational "code golfers" sought the shortest possible quines in their favorite programming languages, and the Cyranos could easily have looked up the optimum example in any such language or found it for themselves.

But in English, the rules were far less precise, and the effects less predictable. The Cyranos had absorbed terabytes of human-written text, but that was poor basis on which to judge edge cases where the language became cramped and potentially cryptic. Vince suspected that each potential solution would need to be run past a human partner to verify that it really did meet all the conditions and would yield the required result.

Mira caught his eye and mouthed something silently, but he couldn't make out the words. He returned a puzzled smile, but before she could repeat the message, the buzzer sounded.

Cybil walked up to the whiteboard and wrote:

X is "X is . Sub X for dot base 36" Sub X for dot base 36

"That's fifty-seven characters," she said. "The reader is told what X is, then performs the requested substitution, putting X in place of the full stop inside itself. That yields the original text without the quotation marks. But to interpret text in base thirty-six by the rules we're given, all punctuation marks are stripped away, so we end up with exactly the same number."

Vince stood. "That's beautiful," he conceded. "It might take a few seconds' thought to interpret, but I don't think the intended audience would find it ambiguous."

He paused, then added, "However . . ." and approached the whiteboard. Cybil frowned but stood aside. Vince picked up a marker and wrote beneath her answer:

Base 62 1jVS4ctnXGKY7hMF1zlPCRMi0B2TUvxSshs2aisu0wu0

"That's fifty-two characters," he said. "When we interpret it in base thirty-six, the lowercase letters become uppercase, but anyone who's been told about that convention would realize, after a few seconds' thought, that the base could also be increased to sixty-two, by treating lowercase letters as twenty-six more digits." He turned to address Cybil. "Do you accept that the third token here, interpreted as base sixty-two, yields the same number as the base thirty-six interpretation of the full text?"

"Yes," she replied. Her tone and demeanor were every bit as gracious as if he'd found something valuable she'd dropped in the street and held it up to her, muddy and soiled, asking if it was hers.

The chief adjudicator said, "Trentham, one point. West Ryde . . . one and a half!" He kept talking—thanking and congratulating people, plugging the recordings of the earlier matches—but the supporters all but drowned out his words.

The Trentham Student Council had laid out tea and scones for everyone at the rear of the hall. As Vince moved between the fold-up tables, he saw Wahid scrolling through an app on his phone.

"They're already pumping out the message that the win says nothing about the real world," Wahid announced gloomily. "Who cares about dot matrix codes from prison cells when you're looking for the most efficient employee?"

"Fuck them," Vince replied. "Have you seen the kind of questions people get asked at interviews?"

"Yeah, fuck them," Wahid agreed. "But I still want to know if I'll ever get hired."

Mira said, "We put one scratch in the Cyranos' paint job. But it's not all down to us. There'll be more."

Vince turned; she and Zach were standing behind him.

"There ought to be some special glasses," Zach mused, surveying the small crowd around them, "that show you all the Cyranos standing beside their partners."

Cybil approached the group. "Could I talk to you for a moment?" she asked Vince.

"Sure."

She gestured that he should accompany her. Vince didn't want to be rude, so he followed, glancing back apologetically at his friends.

When they reached an alcove at the side of the hall, she said, "I've been asked to sound you out about a scholarship."

"Asked by whom?"

"Hyperfine would provide you with a free AI collaborator and cover the fees to attend Trentham or another AI-friendly school."

Vince was bemused. "Don't people usually have their Cyranos installed when they're about five?"

Cybil winced at the vulgar nickname but swallowed her distaste and replied, "That's ideal, but people can adapt well into their teens."

"Honestly," Vince said, "I'm surprised that one close-run quiz in nowhere-ville is such a threat to the company's brand that they'd spend a million dollars to neutralize it. It's also pretty insulting that the offer doesn't cover the whole team . . . but maybe trying to divide us is the whole point."

Cybil smiled. "It's not about any threat. Hyperfine recognizes potential wherever they spot it, and they don't want to see it go to waste."

"Nor do I," Vince replied. "Which is why I'd prefer to keep my skull free of chatter."

"It's not 'chatter,'" Cybil promised him. Her irises were green, but Vince could see a polychromatic shimmer slide across the dark pits of her pupils. "And it's not like the incompetent tutors you're used to, or even the brightest human companion. We've taken sand from the beaches and deserts of the Earth, then melted it down and fashioned it into the substrate for a truly alien intelligence. That intelligence has consumed our own culture and history, the way a larva consumes a leaf, and now it's growing into an entirely new form that will transcend—"

She stopped. Vince was laughing.

"I always thought the Cyranos were meant to be eloquent," he said, once he'd got control of himself. "But . . . seriously? You think you'll win anyone over with that kind of fifth-hand, faux-lyrical babble about 'intelligent sand'? It sounds like you took it straight out of some drug-snorting venture capitalist's podcast."

"You can mock us all you like," Cybil replied icily. "But until you've formed a bond like I have, you'll never know how glorious it is."

"Maybe," Vince conceded. "But from the outside, it's starting to look like your parents gave you a talking teddy bear with an Internet connection and a lot of computing power to play with when you were young, then never got around to telling you that you needed to grow out of pretending it was real."

As he walked back to his friends, the bus driver was already corralling everyone to leave.

"What was it you were trying to tell me before?" Vince asked Mira. While the Trentham team was mesmerized by the search for the shortest English quine, she'd been mouthing . . . some kind of joke? Some acerbic observation on the semantic tar pit they'd built for their opponents?

"I was just telling you not to eat too many scones," Mira replied. "I saw them bringing them out, so I wanted you to leave some room so we could all go for ice cream later."

Vince suddenly recalled the scent of vanilla from his first trials with the Combray. But it had never been allocated to a specific experience; the slot remained free, to be used however he wished.

He said, "Ice cream, to celebrate victory. That sounds good."

ABOUT THE AUTHOR

Greg Egan is an Australian science fiction writer. His latest books are the novel *Morphotrophic* and the collection *Sleep and the Soul*.

Giant Grandmother
LIU MAIJIA, TRANSLATED BY BLAKE STONE-BANKS

The algal-protein reagent oozed from the glass vial and into the tube connected to my arm at a glacial pace. Fixing my gaze on the dense milky elixir, I counted each tick of the clock. The reagent took seven minutes and twenty-eight seconds to reach my body and spin me toward evolution's unknown territories.

Before the reagent infused, however, its flow halted. My preceptor's voice crackled over the loudspeaker: "Purification suspended. Evolution postponed. Ji-Yue, your grandmother has come to visit you."

My preceptor drove me from the lab back to the Residential Zone. The ride wasn't short, but I kept silent the whole way.

"Don't worry," my preceptor reassured. "As long as your evolution completes today, any deviation will be negligible. For twenty-two years, you've proven your diligence and focus. A short break won't trigger an abnormality. The database will automate the necessary adjustments on its own. All is within manageable limits. Don't feel bad about this. When it comes down to it . . . this is your grandmother."

At first glimpse, I thought I was looking at the crimson sunset refracting through the glass gate of the Residential Zone. As we drew closer, however, what had looked like a fiery cloud took on the shape and color of a small mountain. Then, the mountain too began to shift, as the vertebrae arched one by one. The sun's glow highlighted folds and creases branching across the rough skin. A deep sigh rippled over the giant's arched back. The strength in her breath alone would frighten away anyone who might dare challenge her.

I exited the car and stepped cautiously into the giant's shadow.

"How can you be sure it's my grandmother?" I asked, mesmerized by its size, even while sprawled over the dry ground.

"SNP sequencing was conclusive. Besides, you think there's another Asian elephant that would trek through mountains and rivers to find this place and then ask for you by name?" My preceptor glanced at his watch, then hit the switch on the glass gate. "Why don't you go for a walk, give her a tour? After twenty-plus years, I imagine the place has changed quite a bit. I'll pick you up in two hours."

The gears of the glass gate whirled, startling Grandma. Her back clenched. Her head turned, revealing her anxious expression. Compared with the brute strength of her body, her eyes were warm and tender. They circled several times before lowering to fix on mine. She jumped to her feet and rushed forward, stirring up dust. Her trunk froze, motionless, just centimeters from my face.

Her belly had gotten stuck in the gate. Grandma writhed back and forth, calling "A-Ji!"

Instead of answering, I instinctively stepped back. Her gaze faltered, and her trunk drooped, but she managed to steady herself without breaking the gate. Her heaving body deflated slightly. She lifted a front leg and eased forward, the gate's frame scraping across her body. Dry mud and dust flaked from the cracks in her skin until she stood directly in front of me.

"Whoa," I said, full of awe. Mirroring Grandma's upturned trunk, I raised my hand to greet her. "Have you had anything to eat yet? Aunt Shao's café is still open. We could go there and relax."

I led Grandma into the ultraviolet light of the disinfection tunnel. With her following a few steps behind, I shut my eyes, letting intuition guide me. I adjusted my gait, trying to keep a couple meters ahead.

Twenty-two years before, I had been told Grandma was scheduled to evolve, but nothing more. Though there were whispers she might have evolved into an elephant, I didn't learn the truth until her case became public a month later. It was another three years after, when the new edition of *A Contemporary History of Evolution* was published, that I finally saw the security camera image of a large Asian elephant on the verge of bursting through the laboratory wall.

Only now was I seeing the giant with my own eyes. For the first time since that day twenty-two years before, I was with my grandmother again.

I thought about a course I'd taken years before called *New Species, New Moralities*. The professor had built this course around the theme of what he called "reverence for unknown truth." I realized I had no clue how Grandma, from her elephant perspective, might see me after all these years. I intuited, though, that maintaining a physical distance of a couple meters was an appropriate way to express my reverence.

The disinfection tunnel continued on longer than I remembered. When I opened my eyes again, I was surprised to see Grandma now walking ahead of me. I was even more surprised, however, to see several earth-brown patches streaking her back. In the ultraviolet light, only blood had that color.

"Are you hurt?" I called to Grandma.

"Am I?" Grandma gave her trunk a shake. "I probably got scratched by thorns."

There were four Evolution Bases globally, all constructed in un-inhabitable zones, such as undersea or high plateaus. Ours was the primary base, which had been constructed first, deep in the inland desert. Nothing grew for hundreds of miles. There were no thorny shrubs nearby that could have scratched her. The one threat I could think of was that posed by the extremist groups who had entrenched themselves at the desert's edge. Staunchly opposed to the Evolution Project, they had been there since our base was built. Some were true believers driven by opposing visions of technological development. Others were mercenaries funded by gene-mod and pharmaceutical corporations, cloaked as human rights warriors. For years, they had taken turns on the global stage, kicking up one crisis after another. I had no doubt that the wounds on Grandma's back were inflicted by human weapons.

Emerging from the tunnel into the Residential Zone, our view opened onto the broad sunlit square. The towering portraits of Darwin and Mendel were on full display above a line of many smaller, lesser portraits. I glanced at Grandma, searching for a flicker of human emotion as she took in the view. My eyes, however, kept focusing on her bloodstained skin and scars, still earth-brown in the light of day. My attempt at a furtive glance swelled into an unrestrained stare.

Grandma, sensing my concern, changed the subject. "So, Little Zhang is now your preceptor?"

With her teeth and mouth so transformed, Grandma's words were slurred and indistinct—but she had at least retained her ability to speak.

"Yeah," I said, turning to face her. "Professor Zhang's my preceptor. After your evolution, he took on the responsibility of my education. He's now the Evolution Project's chief engineer."

Grandma trumpeted a high-pitched yelp, and her gait perked up. "When he was your grandfather's doctoral student, Little Zhang got scolded plenty. And now he's a chief engineer!" She proceeded through the square, oblivious to when her steps crushed the foliage or toppled trash bins. "Things have really developed. The government poured in quite some money."

Most others were in training this time of day, so few passersby saw the wandering elephant. Those who did see restrained their surprise. Prospective Evolvers were expected to accept the unexpected and even the impossible. After all, the ecological niches awaiting us were uncharted realms. I noticed only one acquaintance, to whom I nodded, but I kept by Grandma's side.

"The early Evolvers provided enough promising data that funding has remained quite good," I told her. "Professor Zhang has been under far less pressure. If my evolution goes smoothly, the government will make the case that there is no longer any reason to fear chromosomal mutation . . . "

"Well, it seems everything is getting better then?" Grandma swung her trunk, then raced forward. "Wow! There's a movie theater here?"

Only when I caught up and put my hand on Grandma's skin did I realize that her hardened hide was layered with fine, prickly hairs. Compared with the brute force of her body, this was an unexpected softness that brought back memories of childhood, when Grandma would hold me tight with her downy gray hair brushing against my neck.

"How nice—it feels now like a place one can truly live. Your grandfather was a strict minimalist. He did everything to forbid such indulgences. We all suffered plenty under his rules."

"Grandpa always held that hardship and struggle were essential to one's character," I said. "His beliefs weren't wrong in the context of that time . . . *With evolution supported by the technology of today, training need not be as harsh as it was in the past.*"

Grandma tilted her head, her huge ears bending forward. "That's a quote from the end of *A Contemporary History of Evolution*, isn't it?"

In her delicate, dark eyes, I caught a familiar flash of emotion that bridged the decades that had separated us. Memories, like bacteria evading the front lines of the immune system, could slip past the barriers of time. Once inside, their growth was exponential.

"Yes, it is. I was flipping through the *History* recently, and it stuck with me . . . " But before I could finish, Grandma set off, galloping toward the cinema.

I glanced up at the clock projected onto the ceiling over the Residential Zone, concerned that Grandma thought we should watch a film together. There was far too little time, even if the theater could accommodate her size. Then suddenly Grandma shouted, "A-Ji, how does this work?"

She was standing utterly confused at the cinema entrance next to the sugar-free ice cream machine, tapping her trunk against its colorful display. The expression on her face was the same as it had been years ago during the third renovation of our base, when my aging grandmother had stared blankly for hours at the world shifting before her. Of course, she had since evolved into another species while I had not, but her expression was the same. The evolutionary gulf Grandma now spanned with ease was, in my mind, a storm of confusion. Observing her from a distance, bound by the certainty of blood and kinship, my thoughts began to unravel. In that moment, the immense figure before me and the memory of my grandmother finally fused into one.

Grandma now stood at 4.2 meters and weighed at least 5,500 kilograms. Her trunk was more flexible, more sensitive, and more versatile than the appendage of any other creature of our time. Over the past twenty-two years, she had had more than enough time to integrate into an elephant family, and with her human neurons still intact, it would have been effortless for her to become their matriarch. She could survive the harshest environments and had virtually no enemies. She was, in every sense, a creature at the apex of the food chain.

Everything I knew about the world beyond base came from news and books, but that was enough to understand our planet had not been improved by our technological progress. Humanity had reached one-tenth the speed of light fifty years ago, yet we had never reached the future we dreamed of. Instead, reckless exploitation of resources, heavy industry, and nuclear pollution, along with unrestrained genetic engineering, had wrecked the human genome. *Fundamentals of Human Genetics* had not been updated in seven years because the rate of chromosomal mutation was too fast to track. At the time the last edition of the book was published, the first sub-band within band 24 on the short arm of chromosome 17 was already extinct, and sixty-seven percent of newborns outside the bases were being born without functioning immune systems.

The exhilaration of humanity's pre-lightspeed era, and the disillusionment that followed, were things I couldn't fully comprehend. Though our base had undergone technological upgrades, we avoided keeping pace with the more advanced forms of automation. This was a way to focus on our own project, as well as a form of resistance against the violence inherent in humanity's expansion.

The incandescent lamps that illuminated the square bathed Grandma in light, highlighting her scars. She had shouldered that bygone era's aggression and loss and now had fought to return through those who had attacked her just to see me. She hardly had space to move without running out of space here. Even something as simple as an ice cream machine left her at a loss. The skin folded around her eyes in an expression of humiliation. Everything here was fragile, as though it could shatter by her mere observation. She was now out of place even in her former home, amidst the project she and my grandfather had built in hopes of opening a path forward for humanity.

This place, which had once belonged to her, now could no longer accept her.

"Alright, what flavor do you want?" I asked.

"Banana!"

I ordered myself a mint chocolate chip cone. By the time I had it in my hand, Grandma had already swallowed her banana cone in a single bite. Her massive trunk now circled my cone to take in its scent. I held it out to her and said, "You should try the mint too."

The machine churned out ice cream just fast enough to keep pace with Grandma's appetite. I sat down next to it, swiping payments with one hand and passing her the finished cone with the other.

"I guess you like it?"

Grandma stepped back and tapped her trunk against the machine with satisfaction. "Simply delicious. The banana is the best."

"Gotcha . . . " I ordered another banana ice cream, then mustering courage, asked, "So what does it feel like, being an elephant?"

"Well, it's alright, I guess."

"Have they stopped monitoring you? My preceptor said that after they released you, they kept watch to ensure you were safe."

"Yes—they stopped that way back. The original reason was that our base satellites got requisitioned for other projects. Later, another Evolver had some particularly interesting results, so Little Zhang and the others decided his telomeres were more valuable, I guess. After that, they more or less stopped paying attention to me."

"Oh, I can guess which Evolver it was—he was a senior who looked after me. The algal-protein reagent used in my round of evolution even contains his telomeres." As I chose which flavor of ice cream to feed her next, I stole another glance at her wounds—though there was little need. I had already memorized every cut and scar on her body. "But it's still dangerous outside. They shouldn't leave you unattended like this."

Grandma's dark, raindrop-shaped eyes froze in place, welled with emotion. "Listen. I'm doing fine, A-Ji. I really am."

"The situation on the outside must be even worse than they say. To which chromosome has the erasure spread? You and Grandpa pointed the path forward for us, and yet there are so many who still wish to harm you?"

The portraits of the scientists—the pioneers of evolution—displayed in the square had become for my generation mere questions on our exams. For Grandma, though, they represented her life choices, her convictions, the blueprint she and Grandpa had bestowed for life on Earth.

When most scientists had focused on how to accelerate the development of powerful technologies, the faction of biologists led by Grandma and Grandpa had dreamed of an alternate future. They insisted civilization could not be crudely ranked by its capacity to harness energy. The true focus of development, they contended, should return to humanity itself—to explore new forms of civilization. Otherwise, the future's promising advancement would, in fact, deliver greater catastrophes. Their voices were faint, and most people ignored them at the time.

Only when chromosome 22 began to vanish across our species did those in power finally understand. Their drive to accelerate to one-fifth and eventually one-half lightspeed had created a Great Filter that threatened to annihilate most of humanity. Despite vocal opposition, the Evolution Project finally began receiving government support. A community of chromosomally stable individuals gathered at our base to live together and train as Evolvers, shaping a viable solution for the failures of genetic engineering. Their vision was that humanity might evolve in a way that allowed us to both transcend our existing chromosomes and preserve our genetic lineage, a shared community within the bounds of carbon-based life.

If a civilization governed by genetic engineering was a dead end, then evolution toward one guided by protein expression might open a path to freedom. This idea, a line my grandmother herself had first said, became our base's founding principle. Even today, few beyond our base believed it.

Looking now upon Grandma's scars, what I felt was neither anger nor distress. I had been trained to regulate dopamine and serotonin levels within a range that never exceeded 0.9 percent. I regarded Grandma calmly now, amused by the smear of banana cream at the corners of her mouth.

"A-Ji, listen to me—compared to true freedom, their threats mean nothing." Grandma's gaze shifted back to the ice cream as she took another lick. "You know, when I first left base, Little Zhang and the others didn't just monitor me, they made me file reports. I never imagined that after evolving into an elephant, I'd still have to work. For the longest time, I worried they'd build some giant keyboard and force me to type them up."

Grandma's exaggerated gestures with her trunk and expression of indignation were comical. I looked down to force back a laugh as I handed her another ice cream.

"But honestly, they should have kept monitoring me—lately I've felt some strange shifts in my body."

"What do you mean?" I asked.

"Everything is growing . . . blurry—my memories of once being human. And yet, the more those memories fade, the more profoundly I feel my sense of belonging to humanity. Isn't that strange?"

"What is the biggest difference between being human and being elephant?"

"Hmm, well . . . I'm not sure I remember exactly what it felt like to be human, but I suppose the difference isn't as profound as one might think. Overall, being an elephant is a bit more comfortable—except when your ass itches, and you can't find a tree."

I broke out laughing. Grandma answered with a playful trumpet of her trunk.

That was my grandmother. Whether human or elephant, she always managed to turn the heaviest of topics into laughter. When I was eight, both my parents evolved, not long after Grandpa, generating precious data for our base and its cause. I became an orphan. Everyone expected my childhood would be a lonely one. Yet with Grandma at my side, I lived a full childhood in every sense—with all the joy and sadness. I weathered the storms of adolescence and its chaotic rush of hormones. I wounded those dearest to me over and again. I flirted with violence and self-destruction. And it was through that destruction and reconstruction that I was able to rebuild myself.

The ice cream machine blinked a message that it was sold out. Grandma pushed the last ice cream back toward me. "Little Zhang said you're evolving today. We don't have long together—maybe we can watch a movie next time."

Her trunk curled around me, lifted me up, and placed me gently at the top of her neck. "Where's Aunt Shao's shop? I'll take you there."

We crossed the square again under the gaze of Darwin, Mendel, and the others who had prepared the foundation for a new evolution driven by free will. Grandma marched past them as though the portraits were of no concern—though her husband, her daughter, her son-in-law, and she herself were among the celebrated portraits.

She had always taught that on this journey to freedom, our human wounds of sorrow and hardship were superficial.

Eating my ice cream on Grandma's back, I looked at the bench where I stopped to gather my thoughts each day, the library where I had done my research, the warehouse that stored the blood and DNA of my grandparents and parents . . . From four meters up, everything in our Residential Zone appeared transformed. Once again, with Grandma's help, I was able to see the base anew. Even as I was about to evolve into another kind of being, I was able to rediscover my own ecological niche from her shoulders.

"A-Ji, why did you choose today for your evolution?"

Grandma didn't know that one's Evolution Day was no longer left to the Evolver to decide. For ease of coordination, recordkeeping, and perhaps even a sense of ceremony, any candidate who passed the strict selection process to qualify for evolution would evolve on their fortieth birthday.

"My hormones are stable, and my compatibility with the algal proteins is higher than anyone else's right now. Every test shows I've reached the psychological maturity required. I'd also say that the hours I've devoted to cultivation and study have hit a saturation point. According to the Project Team—running the unification models of my data against that of earlier Evolvers—I've reached the optimal moment to evolve."

I avoided mentioning that today was also my fortieth birthday. The fact that Grandma didn't bring it up suggested she had forgotten—though perhaps *forgotten* wasn't the right word. Rather, I suspected her sense of time no longer followed human rhythms, but the rhythms of an elephant.

"That so?" Grandma asked. "Then I really did come at just the right time."

"Indeed. My preceptor had to pull me out of the Purification Chamber to see you. If you'd come even an hour later, it would have been too late to see me."

Grandma paused in silence for a full minute before speaking softly: "A-Ji, evolution is not the same as death."

"I know. I remember you telling me that when I was young. My preceptor says that as well. But . . . you've been gone so long, and I waited all these years. I figured I'd never see you again."

"Impossible!"

"Why did you come back only now—after so long?"

"The rainy season lasted longer than usual. The river ran deep, and I couldn't cross it."

"Have you been many places? Where did you go during all this time?"

"Too many to name. Those places in my mind, however, are mapped into my elephant memory—I know where these places are, but I have no means to express it in human language. Elephants draw maps in their minds that guide us on our migrations over vast distances, so we never lose our way. Our memories are extraordinary—ten times stronger than those of humans."

"You carry a memory map of your own?"

"Indeed. That's another feeling growing stronger in me. At first, I thought I was just wandering aimlessly, but later I realized—I was sketching that vast map."

"All this time you've been drawing a map?"

"Yes, but it is a map too large for me to put it into words. Speaking now, I can't quite make out what it really is. No matter how advanced the human brain is with language, there are still limits to what it can comprehend."

"You think the elephant memory map is more advanced than human cognition?"

"More or less. I suppose it would take a more advanced life-form, looking from a higher vantage point, to say for sure. It's one of the things I want to talk about with everyone on this visit."

Time ticked by, and as the clock projected on the Residential Zone's ceiling completed another cycle, Grandma seemed to finally recall the rhythms of human time again. She quickened the pace of both her gait and voice: "A-Ji, are you married?"

"No."

"Do you have children of your own?"

"No, but the Project Team is storing my eggs. Every evolver leaves DNA samples behind. If it turns out that my new niche is broadly adaptable, they might even clone me at scale."

"Wow, you might become the mother of a new breed for humanity?"

"And that would make you grandmother to the new humanity."

"Were I so lucky." She laughed. "Being your grandmother is enough for me, A-Ji." She curled her trunk and caressed my head. Perhaps the trunk's soft, fine hairs stirred a memory of her human years, for her voice, once rough and firm like her skin, softened to a familiar gentleness.

"A-Ji, after today, I expect we may be apart again for some time. I want you to remember that the happiest moments of my life were the day your mother was born and the day you were born. If I'm being honest, the thrill I felt at your birth was even stronger. Even if I forget that someday, the fact will never change."

• • •

When Grandpa was still alive, Aunt Shao assisted in the kitchen of a makeshift laboratory. As our base expanded, she left the laboratory and opened her café in the Residential Zone. Evolver candidates were forced to limit intake of carbohydrates and sugars. Many foods were entirely forbidden to increase evolution success rates. The light snacks from Aunt Shao's café were among the few foods officially approved by the project team.

When we arrived, Aunt Shao was able to accept Grandma's elephant form far more quickly than I had. Perhaps friendship itself was another unknown truth I still couldn't grasp. Beaming, Aunt Shao brought out a large bowl of freshly roasted walnuts to share. She scattered a handful at Grandma's feet, and before Grandma's massive foot even pressed down on them, the shells cracked open, revealing the fragrant nuts inside. Impressed, Aunt Shao tossed more onto the floor in front of us.

Grandma was picking up walnuts one by one and handing them to me, not stopping to eat any herself. Kernels and crumbs clung to the rough folds of her trunk. I was reminded even more of the Grandma I knew in my youth.

From the day I was born until she evolved—and even now, she always helped crack life's hard shells to place its fruits in my hands. Yet in my youth and ignorance, I had complained constantly to her that the fruit was too small and didn't taste as it should. So, for years after I had turned eighteen and Grandma had evolved, I was weighed down by guilt about the years she spent caring for me. I had believed Grandma became that lost elephant because she had missed her optimal age for evolution.

My grandfather had been the pioneer, my parents the successors, and Grandma—like me—had been identified early on for the genetic makeup that qualified her as an Evolver. In fact, she should have evolved much earlier, but when I was a child, she refused to leave me. As I grew up and became more willful and rebellious, Grandma had worried all the more, postponing her evolution several times. By the time I was an adult, Grandma was already seventy-three.

Prior to my grandmother's evolution, high error rates marred the evolution procedures. Back then, the protein reagents that aided evolution were still unstable. Several candidates had evolved into meropenem, an antibiotic that induces extreme resistance, and transformed our base into a petri dish for superbugs. My grandfather, one of the very first, evolved into fungal spores within the primitive, makeshift lab he'd built without considering safeguards. It took his engineers an entire month scanning for brain wave signals before they finally located his spores scattered like dust along the crevices of the lab's ceiling tiles.

Grandma had been first to propose the extraction of algal proteins to assist our evolution. Algae, after all, are among the oldest surviving organisms on this planet, having endured multiple mass extinctions in their own way. The possibilities of life encoded in them proved far greater than we imagined. It was only natural, then, that Grandma became the test subject for the algal-protein reagent. The project's engineers prepared themselves for her to evolve into any conceivable form of life. They never expected that at seventy-three years old, Grandma might evolve into an elephant.

In our *Contemporary History of Evolution* course, my professor once mentioned that the government had been deeply displeased with my grandmother's evolution. Our project nearly collapsed because of it. A human evolving into spores, bacteria, or even a starship was somehow acceptable—but to become an elephant felt more like devolution to those outside our base. Humanity, they insisted, must never devolve into animals. They overlooked that humans had always been animals, and they were oblivious to the fact that various animals were in their ways far more advanced than we were. Working overnight for three days, the entire project team focused on preparing a seventy-three-page report to refute the criticism and vitriol that the outside world had directed our way.

The report contended that my grandmother's evolution marked the first time in history the human mind had effectively influenced gene expression to achieve true biological transformation. With the aid of the algal-protein starter culture and its reagent, this new evolution was rapidly becoming safer and more feasible, opening a path for human individuals to transcend their genetic coding and reassemble their protein sequences. The result of my grandmother's evolution was neither a human-elephant hybrid nor a human merely resembling an elephant—and it certainly was no mere elephant. The experiment had in fact produced a new human species of the elephant genus: *Homo elephantidae*. Evolving into an elephant should not be misconstrued as human devolution. Rather, the elephant form had existed within the subconscious of the Evolver. Though the subconscious selection of an elephant may appear random, this randomness proved the certainty of the subconscious self. Humanity no longer needed to fear the disappearance of chromosomal mutation and deletion. To the contrary, humanity could now evolve from carbon-based organisms into intelligence-driven life.

As new civilizational forms were seeded into Evolvers' subconscious, our species would progress from the expansionist drives of the selfish gene to define a spiritual civilization founded on a new morality.

"What a subject evolves into is irrelevant. It is how we evolve that matters," the report concluded. The experiment was hailed as an unprecedented success that would reshape the future of humanity.

Concerned that my guilt over Grandma's evolution into an elephant was hindering my training, my preceptor shared much of the report's background with me, assuring me that Grandma was in no way a "failed evolution." In fact, much of the report had been prepared under her guidance before her evolution. This knowledge had helped put the twenty-year-old me at ease. Now, seeing and touching Grandma's trunk, wide ears, and sturdy legs, I found myself setting aside this textbook script about the future of humanity. Instead, I leaned into another truth: it wasn't that Grandma evolved into an elephant, but that she had finally evolved into herself.

She was always meant to be the way she was with me now.

She embodied strength, intelligence, and dignity with the full spectrum of emotion. She might seem clumsy in a place too small for her, and with a human granddaughter she had to be so careful with—but that was only because she now belonged to a wider world where she could run free across vast distances.

It was I who had bound her these past eighteen years to being a mere grandmother.

My grandfather had evolved into spores, and my parents into patches of moss—for both of which no form of communication has yet been found. Compared with their fates, Grandma's evolution into an elephant had carried a much higher chance of potential for communication with humans. In those decades apart, I often wondered if I would ever be able to ask her: Why an elephant? What exactly had the starter culture of algal-protein reagents done inside her body? I never believed that randomness was anything more than a safe, convenient explanation by the higher-ups. Grandma had always wielded a power of wisdom that refused to leave her fate to chance.

On the day of our reunion, however, I never asked that question. Grandma, in high spirits, spent our remaining hour sharing her experiences in the warmth of the spring sun, the feeling at the arrival of the monsoon, the feel of green shoots beneath her footsteps in moonlight, the sunrise vistas crossing the Yunnan-Guizhou Plateau, and the encompassing green embrace of rainforests. I listened intently as an elephant described the world from her perspective, a world so profoundly different from mine. Compared with this, the answer to my question was insignificant.

Grandma and I walked back to the gates of the Residential Zone where a group of engineers were tinkering with their instruments and straightening newly raised tents. From the looks of it, I could tell they were preparing to run tests on her, perhaps to discuss the discoveries she had made on the outside. Both of us had matters to attend to on our own. Without a word, we knew our reunion had reached its end.

I was still gathering the words for a farewell when Grandma stepped through the gate. The night sky surrounding our base was now dark. I hadn't brought a jacket, yet I did not feel cold—only the numb sting of the wind against my cheek as we lingered by the gate. Outside, Grandma circled once, as if something had just come back to her. Before the doors could close, Grandma leaned her head back inside. Her trunk encircled me and pulled me close. Pressed against my shoulder, she sighed deeply, imprinting me onto that memory map that only an elephant carries.

"A-Ji," she said, "I'd love more than anything to give you some guidance before your own evolution. And yet, I fear to do so would be a betrayal of the faith I have in you. The truth is, I myself have forgotten what truly happened in that instant of change. But there is something I do want to leave with you, which is this. Your grandfather and I, your preceptor, and thousands of evolution researchers poured every human, material, and financial resource into freeing us from the instincts that once ruled us, so that our intellect and imagination might carve out new futures. That, beyond question, is a positive advancement. Yet we cannot deny that our human wisdom and memory is etched into our genes. If one day you do become some higher form of life, and you feel your human genetic code trying to wrest back control . . . you need not rush to resist it. Simply, try to understand it. Then, respect it."

Her trunk's embrace squeezed tighter and released. "That code carried humanity through hundreds of thousands of unforgiving years. Our first niche on this Earth was cut open by their strength."

My preceptor drove me back to the lab.

"So, how was it?" my preceptor broke the silence. "Two hours was no doubt too short. I wish you could have stayed longer. Although at forty, the exact day of evolution makes little difference, if I made an exception for you, the year-end audit would be messy and . . . "

"I'm happy," I told him. "Being happy is enough."

Through the rearview mirror, my preceptor's gaze fell on me. "Ji-Yue, you're looking more and more like your grandmother."

"Yeah, I know."

"You hold your composure just as she did. That's a strength."

"That's only because I'm too happy. In human years, Grandma would be ninety-three now. Under normal circumstances, we would never have had the chance to speak as we did today. Those two hours are already a bonus. And when I think about how, in elephant years, she's only twenty-two—still so young and healthy—I feel truly happy for her."

"You and your grandmother will cross paths again," he said. "I'm sure of it."

"I know. That's why I didn't need to tell Grandma how happy I was. And even if my evolution does not achieve an ideal state, and I can no longer communicate with you, with her, that is a fate I am willing to accept."

My preceptor swiped open the door to the lab.

"Ji-Yue, over the years, I've escorted thirteen groups of Evolvers to the top floor. What happens on one's Evolution Day has no known effect on the outcome, which is why I feel I can say things I normally wouldn't tell you." We stepped into the elevator together, and he pressed the button for the sixteenth floor. "In the most classic theories of evolution, there is no such thing as success or failure, no distinction between what is ideal and what is not. In evolution, only one thing matters."

"What?"

"Diversity."

"Biological diversity?"

"That's right."

"Your evolution today is no different from a launch into the cosmos. Once you've broken free of Earth's gravity, no direction is wrong or right. The universe is vast, the unknown endless—so every path is the right path." The elevator came to a stop, the doors slid open, and the white gate to the evolution lab appeared. "From here, every step you take—if it is chosen by your heart and will—is a step forward for humanity . . . That's something your grandmother told me once."

The evolution lab opened before me. Just ten paces remained before I left the realm of *Homo sapiens*.

My preceptor gestured for me to take the first step. I left the elevator, and he followed.

"When I was a doctoral student," he said, "I asked your grandmother what the ultimate purpose of human evolution was. If it were about countering the threat of chromosomal mutation, then why wasn't the most reliable solution to advance genetic engineering technology to repair the code vanishing from our chromosomes? At the least, that seemed far more ethical than conducting the evolution experiments on human volunteers."

"What did she say?"

"Your grandmother said that we should not define morality from the standpoint of human beings, but from the standpoint of nature itself. In nature, there is no such thing as moral or immoral evolution. If anything, it's that the entire natural world is a stepping stone—a sacrifice for progress. In her view, humanity cannot allow itself to become a cold yet powerful species. Even if we framed our project with the grandest intentions, there was still a measure of human self-interest inherent to the vision."

I paused at the threshold of the Purification Chamber, seizing my last chance for a question. "What kind of self-interest?"

"I guess she wanted to prove human life, in every form, could achieve its true potential. Your grandmother is happy. Today, she saw that you are happy too. It's likely she has already shared with you a better answer than I can give."

My mentor nodded, and I stepped alone into the Purification Chamber.

"Well then, Ji-Yue—evolve with courage!"

Seven minutes and twenty-eight seconds later, evolution arrived right on time.

The process could hardly be called a comfortable one. How to breathe, how to control my muscles, how to seal the mind to maintain my neural structures—I had practiced these countless times in my training simulations and mastered them. Yet when the evolution truly began, the feeling was unlike anything I had experienced in a simulation.

It was as if I could see the mass of algal-protein cultures blooming inside me, an invisible force flooding every neuron and nerve cell. The rush of vertigo that followed almost drowned me. It was a roller coaster through some unknown dimension in endless free fall or being pulled to the surface from the ocean's most profound depths.

I penetrated the surface and drew in breath, though I could not feel the rise or fall of my lungs.

The world rushed in from every direction, filling my entire field of vision.

It seemed instantaneous—or rather, that a great length of time had been accelerated into a single moment.

All I knew was that on the first day of my forties, I had become a new species under the genus *Homo*. As for what species I was, what form I had taken—where I had budded on the tree of evolution or whether my evolution may help humanity toward a better future—those were questions for my preceptor and others to answer.

All I could do in that moment was simply feel the world, to strain my being to inhabit this new niche and translate even the smallest sensation into a form of knowledge that might still be comprehensible to humankind.

All deviations are within manageable limits.
All unknowns are open to exploration.
All loneliness is surmountable.

The sole anomaly occurred precisely at the moment my evolution completed.

Countless information streams unfolded across the field of my vision, coalescing into a map drawn across the vastness of our planet. It was a gift wrapped up long ago by some higher species. There could be no doubt it was intended for my evolution, for me alone—for what other elephant would engrave my name upon this map. It read simply:

Happy birthday, A-Ji.

We are merely travelers in the Laniakea Supercluster, strung into line by our shared alleles like the synchronized hands of a clock. We part ways, yet always find each other again, entwined as we reach into the future, return to the past, embed each other in light, sky, and these folds of earth.

Originally published in Chinese in *Xingun (Nebula) Awards XIV*, Sichuan Publishing House of Science and Technology, 2024.

Translated and published in cooperation with Storycom and *Science Fiction World*.

ABOUT THE AUTHOR

A young writer and member of the China Writers Association, **Liu Maijia** graduated from The University of Western Australia with an M.A. in economics. She launched her science fiction writing journey in 2022. The following year, Maijia was nominated for the Chinese Nebula (Xingyun) for Best New Writer and Galaxy Award for Best Novella. In 2024, she was honored as Best

New Science Fiction Writer by the inaugural Tianwen Chinese Science Fiction Literature Contest. In 2025, she was selected for the Science-Fiction Literature Excellence Award at the Third Science Fiction Planet Competition.

Blake Stone-Banks is a translator of Chinese speculative fiction. He speculates in his own fiction too. Born in Kentucky and domesticated in Beijing, he thrives on bluegrass and revolutionary model operas.

The Job Interview

CARRIE VAUGHN

To: Navcom Supervisor Rinzelli
From: Crew Chief Jang
Priority: Urgent

Hi Lisle. Hope you've had some coffee. The topside comms array is still glitching, and engineering hasn't lifted a finger to run diagnostics. They say the work order has to come from your end. Shouldn't take long once they get it. Happy simulated morning to you!

To: Crew Chief Jang
From: Navcom Supervisor Rinzelli
Priority: Urgent

It's always something. I sent that work order yesterday. That would be just like life on Roth Station, to have the work order to fix the comms get swallowed by the glitch in comms. I'll walk down there if I have to. Thanks for the warm greetings. I'll have you know I read your memo before coffee and lived to tell the tale.

Lisle only spent about fifteen minutes trying to contact the engineering department. Her messages bounced, and her vidcom request received an automated out-of-office response. *Someone* had to be there, the engineering department was staffed at all hours for emergencies just like this. Not that this was an emergency, yet. Her job was to keep it from becoming one. She could spend an hour chasing the work order from her station, but it would likely be faster just going there herself, so true to her word—or threat—she marched down to engineering because apparently that was the only way to learn what was actually happening over there.

Roth Station was a rotating drum. Ops and engineering were on the same level, but on opposite sides. The debate, to go through the center or to walk around the ring corridor, was mostly philosophical. Between dealing with shifting gravity through the center or traversing the longer distance around the ring, the two routes took roughly the same amount of time. Lisle usually picked the center route just because she was less likely to run into people she didn't want to talk to.

It was also meditative, floating through the center core and imagining just for a moment that she was somewhere else. In deep space, on a scout ship, maybe. Someplace where no one nagged her about unfinished work orders because the work *just got done.*

She hauled herself down the ladder past the hub where gravity returned and planted her feet firmly on the corridor's mat. Engineering was down a passage and through a hatch. These were the utilitarian areas of the station, with spare lighting and unpainted walls, and signage that was more practical than aesthetic. Truthfully, Lisle found the lack of any decoration comforting. This was about the work, not about appearances.

She arrived at the engineering section. The hatch to the workstation stood open, which she took as an invitation.

Gelbart, Engineering Supervisor, was at the center console, eating what looked like a sandwich straight out of the celo wrapper and getting crumbs all over the monitor deck. One of his underlings was at another console, head propped on hand, staring at a display and occasionally punching a button for no discernible reason.

She paused at the hatchway, waiting for them to notice her. They did not.

"Hi," she said finally. Still chewing, Gelbart calmly looked up. The underling flinched, then tried to look busy, leaning intently over the console.

"Rinzelli," Gelbart said by way of greeting, his mouth half full.

"You should have gotten a work order from me yesterday? I've been trying to find out what happened to it."

"Work order?" His brow furrowed.

"Yeah."

"About what?"

"Glitchy comms. Mainly the topside comms array, but we might be having problems with internal comms as well." She repeated some calming aphorisms to herself before adding, "I tried to call you, but didn't get an answer. I'm glad there wasn't an emergency taking up your attention."

"You called?"

"I got an out-of-office auto-response." Calmly, always calmly. Gelbart looked over his shoulder. "Bez?"

"Huh? Oh. I must have forgotten to take it down after the thing."

What thing? Lisle wondered but knew better than to ask.

She tried again. "I just need to know the status of the work order to run diagnostics on the comms array."

Gelbart shook his head, and her heart sank. "We didn't get it."

"Okay," she said. "I'll send it again—"

"We didn't get it because all work orders need to be routed through the station supervisor's office."

That didn't make any sense. "Since when?"

"Order's right here." He tapped one of his monitors, and she went to read over his shoulder.

To: All Section Sub-supervisors
From: Station Chief Supervisor Morganstern
Priority: Double Urgent

To better facilitate efficient management of station resources and workflow, all work order requests to any department must first be submitted to the office of the Station Chief Supervisor. Effective immediately. Direct inquiries to Assistant Chief Supervisor's Office.

She'd never seen this order. Did everyone get this but her? The address list was hidden, so that didn't tell her anything. Was she left off intentionally, or was this part of the comms glitch? Was this a software problem, a hardware problem, or an office politics problem? She was really beginning to hate this place. Scratch that. She was nearing the end of hating this place. Something was going to give soon.

This used to be a great job. She used to love it here at Roth, a scrappy little mining transfer outpost that was big enough to be interesting but small enough to know just about everyone and really be able to get her hands dirty. She'd learned a lot at this job, but that was under the old station supervisor, Kearney, and his team. Then he'd retired, the new supervisor came in, and . . . Well. Lisle was the last of the old station supervisory crew still standing. Everyone else had quit. She was the only one brave or stupid enough to stick with it.

"So to clarify," she said, "You won't run the diagnostic without getting a work order from Morganstern. Even with me standing right here asking for it."

"Hey, I don't make the rules." He brushed crumbs off the front of his uniform jacket.

"Thanks," she said curtly and walked out.

She had become suspicious. She hated that she had become suspicious.

Her workstation was isolated, in a compartment a couple branches off the main ops corridor and closer to the outer hull, where she could get inputs for various communications systems. She also had a tiny viewport that looked out across Roth's exterior. Sometimes, when the station was rotated toward the dark, she caught herself staring out, watching the blinking lights of satellites and arrays, planetary shuttles, and incoming transports against the backdrop of distant stars, in a longing daze, with a desire to be anywhere but here.

Most of the other section supervisors had their stations clustered toward the forward end of the station, with its more prestigious views and accommodations. Had she been excluded from the memo on purpose, or did the chief supervisor's office just forget she was there? Didn't matter; she was here to do a job, not speculate on the motivation of others.

The Assistant Chief Supervisor was a guy named Mel Dirk. He'd been hired to replace the previous assistant who quit after just a month of working with Morganstern.

To: Assistant Chief Supervisor Dirk
From: Navcom Supervisor Rinzelli
Priority: Urgent

This morning, I discovered that I have not been receiving procedural memos—Gelbart just informed me of the memo stating that all work orders should be directed to the Station Supervisor office. I'd appreciate it if you could check into why I haven't been receiving recent memos, and also, please forward me any important recent memos I might have missed? Much appreciated.

Attached please find the work order requesting a diagnostic of the topside nav array, which should be completed before any interruptions in communication become critical.

Lisle moved on to the rest of her work queue. Busy, but not onerous. Some scheduling issues with the staff, approving an inspection rota for internal comms. She might move that up the priority list. An incoming message beeped her out of her flow.

To: Navcom Sub-supervisor Rinzelli
From: Assistant Chief Supervisor Dirk
Priority: Double Urgent

Hey there! Sorry for confusion. It seems the job title on your messaging ID is wrong. Memos are filtered by job title. Yours didn't get updated to the new designation, and you just slipped through. Mea culpa! I've fixed it now, should be good.

Also: I believe the content of your previous memo rated a Double Urgent Priority label. Cheers!

She had to double check the message header to figure out what he meant by updated job titles, and for a long time, she just stared. Sub-supervisor? *Sub-supervisor?* Turned out she didn't get the memo about that, either.

Her title was Navcom Supervisor. It had always been Navcom Supervisor. It was the job she'd been hired for three years ago. Who changed it? Why? This didn't make sense. The explanation was going to take more than two lines of a memo. She requested a video meeting.

Dirk's face appeared on the monitor. He made an effort to act younger than he was—a slick haircut, his uniform collar jauntily open, smile plastered thick. Skin strangely plasticized with spa treatments. Right now, it appeared stretched in a picture of shock. "Lisle? What's wrong? What's happening?"

"Nothing's wrong."

"Something must be wrong. You're using vidcom."

"It's easier than a memo," she said.

"No one uses vidcom. Memos are standard—"

"Dirk. Why the change in job titles? Sub-supervisor? Really?"

The tension drained away into an expression of self-assured ease. "Right. Ellen thought it was confusing, the section heads and station head all being called supervisor. She thought this would make the organizational structure more clear."

Funny, nobody ever got confused when Kearney was station supervisor. But Ellen Morganstern wasn't Kearney. Ellen Morganstern wanted everyone to call her by her first name because she believed doing so promoted a friendlier working environment.

"I must have missed that memo," Lisle said flatly.

"Yeahhhh," Dirk drawled. "Sorry about that."

"Just so long as I'm looped in from here out."

"Of course, of course." He glanced at another monitor, distracted. "Well then, I'll let you go!"

She started to thank him again out of politeness, but he logged off. Back to the memo mines.

To: Station Supervisor Morganstern
From: Navcom Sub-supervisor Rinzelli
Priority: Urgent

Hi Ellen, I hope you're having a good morning. I understand that work orders are now being routed through your office. I've attached a work order that I sent to engineering yesterday to run diagnostics on a comm array that's been having problems. It should probably be looked at sooner rather than later. Thank you.

She hit *send* and hoped that this would be the last she had to think of it. Engineering would get the work order, run the diagnostics, the glitch would get fixed, all would be well. She was also very aware that this would probably not be the end of it. She couldn't tell if the cramping in her stomach was lunchtime hunger or simmering rage.

Fortunately, she was able to get through a whole raft of entirely normal, mundane tasks like equipment requisitions and staffing reviews. Since Morganstern came on board, Lisle had made an extra effort to record good reviews for her staff, to cover them if and when the chief supervisor's staffing ambitions spread past the supervisor organizational level. No undeserving demotions would happen on Lisle's watch. Except for her own, evidently.

To: Navcom Sub-supervisor Rinzelli
From: Cargo Crew Chief Elleston
Priority: Double Urgent

Hey Lisle. Did you get my memo about problems with the topside comms array? I sent it two days ago. Thing is glitching. Here's what I'm getting from traffic control.

Attached to this was a copy of a memo that was all garbled text, dropped letters, and coding symbols that made Lisle's eyes cross. Even the sender and recipient lines were mush. In a moment of pure whimsy, she wondered if it might be a secret code, and if so, what it said. Maybe: *you need to find a new job.*

It wasn't code, it was a mashed comms system. Too bad internal comms weren't glitching; if Morganstern couldn't read all those memos she insisted on reviewing, she might get on that work order a little faster.

To: Cargo Crew Chief Elleston
From: Navcom Sub-supervisor Rinzelli
Priority: Urgent

Hey Sue. I'm sorry, I didn't. I suspect this has something to do with a recent request that all work orders get routed through Morganstern's office. Did you get that memo? I just found out about it this morning.

I've submitted a priority request for a diagnostic on the array, we should get this nailed down soon. Thanks for letting me know.

Notifications immediately pinged another message coming in.

To: Navcom Sub-supervisor Rinzelli
From: Assistant Chief Station Supervisor Dirk
Priority: Double Urgent

Hey there! The Station Supervisor's office has received your work order regarding diagnostics on the topside comms array. Chief Supervisor Morganstern has questions about whether this particular comms array falls under our jurisdiction or is not instead the responsibility of Trade Guild Systems Division? Given that it handles off-station comms. Could you please submit the information regarding the proper jurisdiction? We wouldn't want to spend resources that should be part of another organization's budget, haha!

This array was how Roth Station communicated with . . . with everyone. All incoming and outgoing comms transmissions routed through there. The station couldn't manage flight traffic without that array. Why would it be Trade Guild SysDiv's problem? Roth was part of an independent mining operation; Trade Guild had a single two-person office here handling mining regulations and cargo inspections. Lisle did not want to spend her afternoon sorting through organizational documents. This was *stupid*.

One solution occurred to her. A Gordian knot kind of solution, slicing right through the entire bureaucracy in one fell swoop.

To: Station Supervisor Morganstern
Cc: All Section Sub-supervisors
From: Navcom Sub-supervisor Rinzelli
Priority: Urgent

I hereby submit my resignation from the position of Navcom Sub-supervisor of Roth Station, effective immediately. Thank you.

She didn't send this memo. Instead, she hid it away in an unmarked data cache where she put everything she wanted to keep off the network. She'd thought about quitting before this, when she realized she was the last of Kearney's old staff still standing. Writing an actual resignation memo was as close as she'd gotten.

Wasn't as cathartic as she was hoping. Given the situation with the topside comms array, she probably wouldn't be able to leave Roth even if she did quit. As she saw it, she had two options. Find the documentation Dirk was asking for, or go out to the comms array and run the diagnostics herself. Maybe she could find a more appropriate compromise.

And then things got worse.

To: Navcom Sub-supervisor Rinzelli
From: Alice Mining Corp Director Blakely
Priority: Double Urgent

Lisle, I might have a situation here. As a precaution, I'd like to double ore shipments through the afternoon. Please arrange cargo docks and crews and transmit traffic authorizations as soon as possible.

Well, wasn't that something. The mining operation on Alice 3, the planet Roth Station served as a hub for, had always had issues, everything from unstable geology to labor disputes. Blakely wasn't one to panic or catastrophize, so whatever was going on must have been serious. A thrill bubbled up in the back of Lisle's mind. Something interesting. A *challenge*.

She briefly wondered if Blakely would answer his vidcom, but she didn't want to interrupt whatever he was in the middle of. As curious as she was, her job right now wasn't to figure out what was going on; it was getting docks ready for the new shipments.

That was going to be way more difficult without the topside array. Well. They'd just have to make it happen anyway.

To: Alice Mining Corp Director Blakely
From: Navcom Sub-supervisor Rinzelli
Priority: Double Urgent

Understood. Please be advised, we've been having problems with the topside comms array, which will affect traffic control. We're working to resolve the issue before it becomes critical.

This gave her a good reason to prod engineering into action, which she promptly did. Or at least, attempted to do.

To: Engineering Sub-supervisor Gelbart
From: Navcom Sub-supervisor Rinzelli
Priority: Double Urgent.

Under Section 4, Line 12 of the Roth Station Code of Maintenance Regulations, I'm independently authorizing the work order to run diagnostics. This is a time-sensitive situation in which the normal flow of communications has been disrupted, and to maintain station functions, work must be implemented immediately.I'll submit the explanatory forms momentarily.

Lisle allowed herself a moment of pride. How very satisfying, implementing a job the way it was supposed to be done. Next thing was to complete all the forms needed to cover her ass for going behind the back of the supervisor's office. Though it did occur to her—would Morganstern and Dirk even notice? She was excited to find out.

Gelbart responded almost immediately, which gave her a sinking feeling because he never did anything immediately.

To: Navcom Sub-supervisor Rinzelli
From: Engineering Sub-supervisor Gelbart
Priority: Double Urgent

I'm afraid I'll have to forward your request to Station Supervisor Morganstern to confirm the time-sensitive situation designation. Please stand by.

She would not please stand by. This was a space station with five hundred residents that served as a transit hub for a mining colony of ten thousand, and they were inexorably edging toward crisis. Which would require filling out even *more* documentation, and she wanted to avoid that.

For the second time that day, Lisle hauled herself to the engineering department, and not even the liminal, low-g turnover at the hub could calm her down. Storming the last stretch of corridor before engineering, she almost collided with a couple of techs and managed to mumble apologies rather than yelling that they should be working on the comms array. They were internal systems techs; they wouldn't know anything about comms.

One of them stopped and did an actual double take at her. "Supervisor! Ma'am! Crew Chief Jang's looking for you."

"Is this about the topside comms array?" she asked, mid-stride, turning to face him.

"No? I mean, yes, but not just that." He was a young guy, full of polish with brown puppy-dog eyes, bouncing on his toes, eager to get the words out. "This is about traffic monitoring."

"Another glitch?" That was fine. Why not pile on the problems and deal with everything at once?

"Maybe. Traffic control reported an anomaly on the sensors, but given the glitches in the array, they thought it might be a ghost, part of the same malfunction. They're getting error codes."

This wasn't a normal systems glitch. Her instincts were usually pretty good, and a giant flashing red alarm went off in the back of her brain: something much bigger was going on here.

"Right, okay," she told the tech, steeling herself. "I'm on the comms array. Blakely is sending us more traffic, so we'll need to clear docks for him. If we have to do it the old-fashioned way with manual signal relays, then we will."

"You want me to send Chief Jang the memo about that?"

She sighed with relief. "Yes. Please. Thank you. I'll recommend you for all the promotions if you do that."

He smiled happily. "Ma'am."

That poor kid, he was setting himself up for a lifetime of solving other people's problems, just like she had.

In engineering, Gelbart was at his workstation, staring at monitors and eating what appeared to be an entirely different sandwich than the one he'd been eating just a couple of hours earlier. That one had been on a brownish whole wheat-style bread. This one appeared to be on some kind of yeasty roll. Had Lisle eaten lunch today? She couldn't remember. The tech from earlier was at a different workstation, staring at a different monitor. She still couldn't tell exactly what he was doing.

"Gelbart?"

The tech flinched at the edge in her voice. Jumpy guy, wasn't he? Gelbart merely glanced up. Her presence here seemed to evoke no emotional response.

"Gelbart, we need to fix that comms array, now."

"Then get that work order—"

"I'm overriding the work order request under Section 4—You know what? Never mind." She marched over to an empty workstation, logged in her credentials, and took over the entire engineering workflow. Red lights flashed on a couple of monitors; she didn't care.

Gelbart dropped the sandwich and stood. "You can't do that!"

In terms of basic capability, she very well could do it. But he wasn't talking about skills. He was talking about permissions and boundaries and hierarchies and, in those terms, she was way, way out of line.

She wasn't thinking about hierarchies, permission, Roth Station management, or the bottom line of the Alice Mining Corporation.

She just wanted things to run the way they were supposed to. And she didn't want anyone to get killed because things weren't working right.

"It turns out you can do pretty much anything if you're willing to face the consequences," she said with weaponized cheerfulness.

It took just five minutes to get the diagnostics started. She gave priority to the topside array, then the traffic system, and, for good measure, scheduled diagnostics for everything else in case some buggy code had gotten loose in the whole system. If the problem was in the software, she could upload patches to get them through the day, then set up a whole system reboot when they had some time.

While she waited, she routed her messages to this workstation and braced for what she had missed in the last thirty minutes. A whole raft of memos had piled up telling her everything she already knew, but with increasing levels of urgency as the problems compounded. Blakely's shipments were en route, Cargo was scrambling to make room for them, traffic control was screaming—the sensor ghost was still there, and control had just sent out drones to get a real-time visual on what might or might not be out there.

Then a new alert, glowing an adversarial scarlet, landed.

To: Station Supervisor Morganstern
Cc: All Section Sub-supervisors
From: Alice Mining Corp Director Blakely
Priority: Double Urgent Code Red

This is an emergency declaration. We have a full-on labor strike on the surface. Directorial staff is locked in our offices. Internal comms shut down. Please alert the company, please advise.

Almost simultaneously, another angry red alert landed.

To: Navcom Sub-supervisor Rinzelli
From: Crew Chief Jang
Priority: Double Urgent Code Red

Lisle, check the traffic feed.

Lisle had never seen a Double Urgent Code Red classification before, and here she had two of them in a row. The messages glowed faintly, hypnotically. Then she had to actually focus on what was happening. The labor situation on Alice 3 had finally boiled over. Okay. That was Morganstern's responsibility, though the odds of Morganstern actually doing anything . . . Lisle put that thought aside for the moment and did as Jang asked. This sounded like the traffic feeds were working again. If so, why the Double Urgent Code Red priority? She checked the feed, and the situation immediately clarified.

A gunship was screaming toward Roth, burning hard to slow its approach. It might or might not crash into them. This might have been a scare tactic. It was working.

Not a sensor ghost. Not a software glitch. The array had been flooded with bad code. The malfunctions, the blind spots—it had all been sabotage, to keep the station blind and off-balance while the ship entered the system and came at them without warning. At the same time as the labor situation on Alice 3 burst its seams. Interesting.

Lisle didn't know what to do. Her mental flowchart of actions had no branch for this. While she thought she ought to panic, a quiet part of her mind murmured, *thank goodness*. Very soon, Roth wouldn't be her problem anymore. It was a strange, weightless relief.

Then she thought of one thing she might do. It might be very stupid. At this point, anything was worth a try.

To: Incoming Gunship
From: Roth Station Navcom Sub-supervisor Lisle Rinzelli
Priority: Extreme

To the incoming gunship targeting my space station. Can you please identify yourselves and your purpose so that we might perhaps come to an understanding before anyone gets hurt? Thank you.

The message needed time to travel the distance—the quickly diminishing distance—between the station and ship. Lisle thought she might explode, waiting for the minutes to tick down.

And then—

To: Roth Station Navcom Sub-supervisor Rinzelli
From: Trade Guild Military Division Independent Operations Courier *Visigoth*

Priority: Calm Down

Glad to make contact. We are here to conduct an audit of labor conditions on Alice 3, at the request of the Mining Labor Union. Please prepare docking space and good manners. Have a nice day.

So—sabotage, conspiracy. What an exciting day this had turned into. The *Visigoth* had had inside help—of course it had. While she might have loved accusing Morganstern or Dirk, she honestly didn't think they had it in them. The solution was a little more obvious than that.

To: Trade Guild Customs Outpost Director
From: Navcom Sub-supervisor Rinzelli
Priority: Triple Urgent Priority Red

Are those your people coming in hot?

They might as well have been waiting for her message, with their reply already prepared.

To: Navcom Sub-supervisor Rinzelli
From: Trade Guild Customs Outpost Director
Priority: Green

I've been waiting for you to contact us. Please stand down for labor conditions audit.

She sent a vid request because this seemed like the appropriate situation for one. When the call was accepted, Lisle took a moment to breathe deeply, settle herself, and put on a smile. A tense grimace of a smile. But at least she wasn't yelling.

The tag on the vid image said the man was named Elgar. Lisle didn't remember ever meeting him before but recalled his approval codes on a number of communications from Cargo. Unassuming in a dark suit, standard business professional polish, he could pass unnoticed in a crowd. Probably the idea. It was obvious he wasn't part of station personnel because he wasn't anxious or confused. Far from being annoyed at the vid request, he smiled as if pleased.

"Supervisor Rinzelli, how are you?"

Murderous, she thought. "I have to admit, Mr. Elgar, I'm a bit thrown off my game today."

"I imagine you are."

She tried to find a polite, professional way to follow up, and simply couldn't. Moreover, she didn't much care anymore. "If you people wanted to run an audit, why didn't you alert management?"

Elgar was serene. At least someone was enjoying himself. "I think you know the answer to that."

She didn't even have to think about it. "Morganstern never responded to requests."

Oh yeah, he was definitely enjoying himself. "On the other hand, in some situations, surprise audits give us the best results. Can we count on your cooperation, Supervisor?"

"Will it get Morganstern thrown out?"

"I can neither confirm nor deny."

"Thank you for your candor. You have a nice day."

"You as well." He signed off.

Another flurry of memos. One to Crew Chief Jang and Cargo confirming docking space for the TGS MilDiv *Visigoth*. She set up auxiliary comms channels so traffic could clear the space around Roth. Provided her approval for any and all authorizations.

Fascinating, watching the *Visigoth's* entirely efficient operation. Even as they decelerated for docking without crashing into anything, they were arranging shuttle transport to the surface, sending orders to Blakely and the mining operation, and infiltrating all of Roth's internal networks to take command of the station. Technically, part of Lisle's job was trying to stop them, but she had become strangely fatalistic about the whole operation.

She had one more task before the hammer dropped on them.

She'd once come across an old phrase that had resonated with her. "Girding one's loins." Originally, it referred to an ancient style of clothing that normally draped around the legs but could be tied up around the hips in a crisis, when one needed to work. Or fight. The phrase spoke to preparation, to putting on a sort of armor. Signaling that a particular situation was about to get . . . difficult.

Lisle girded her loins, metaphorically, and marched around the next bend in the station's curve to the supervisor's office. In the corridors, people were running. Hatches were slamming shut. No alarm had sounded, there was no outward sign of the impending crisis, but word had spread, and everyone knew. Everyone would have to take care of themselves. Where else could any of them go? But for her, this had become personal.

As she arrived at the closed hatch of the supervisor's office, Mel Dirk slipped out the next door over and got in her way. "Hey hey hey," he said, smirking. "The Chief Supervisor is a little busy right now."

"I bet she is," Lisle said.

"Wait—I don't think—"

Lisle tapped her emergency authorization on the comm panel and opened the hatch.

Ellen Morganstern was at her console, her gaze ratcheting between three different monitors. She was impeccably dressed in a suit of some expensive, silky material that Lisle couldn't have afforded on her salary and would have thought would be difficult on the Chief Supervisor's salary. A riddle for another time. The middle-aged woman looked permanently startled by life in general, eyes wide, asking, *What, who, me?*

Lisle announced. "Ma'am? We've got incoming hostiles." And didn't that sound ridiculously cinematic?

Morganstern glanced up. Her hand went to her chest; her eyes widened even more. "Yes, I can see that."

Dirk came in and set himself by the doorway. Arms crossed, practically vibrating. Lisle was hemmed in. It only made her angry.

"What's your plan?" Lisle asked. Lisle honestly didn't know what would happen, what Morganstern would say. Would she get defensive? Make excuses?

The Chief Supervisor folded her hands on the desk and met Lisle's gaze. "I, for one, am curious why you didn't know about this ahead of time and work to prevent it. Shouldn't you have been tracking in-system communications?" Her gaze went to Dirk; an eyebrow twitched.

"Any anomaly in traffic control should have been flagged, don't you think?" Dirk added, with a determined nod.

All Lisle's communications—or attempts at communications—were logged. That wouldn't matter. They'd dig in and tell their own story. She could get angry, get defensive—they wanted her to get defensive, to stammer denials, give them a guilty-sounding crack they could break open and shove all the blame into.

Fine, she'd take it.

She took one last look at Morganstern's glass-like refusal to react, and Dirk's smarm. "You all have a nice day, why don't you?"

Dirk lobbed a few parting shots, something about unfriendly work environments and overstepping boundaries. She ignored him.

She marched to her own workstation, stored a copy of all her comms transcripts, and sent that resignation memo. Finally, at last. A weight lifted, even though all her authorizations and access would likely be cut off immediately, leaving her trapped on Roth in the middle of a hostile takeover. Not that that would mean anything anyway, when the Trade Guild ship got here.

The ship was probably already here. And she wanted a front row seat.

She wasn't sure what it meant that everyone she ran into, from custodial techs on up to section heads, stopped her to ask what was going on. Did she somehow look like she knew what she was doing? Instead of telling them that she had resigned and officially had nothing to do with anything, she held on to her professional demeanor. The crew didn't deserve this any more than she did. Well, most of them didn't.

"Trade Guild is launching an external labor audit. I recommend cooperating. Just be patient." Her smile felt strained to breaking but must have imparted some reassurance. People seemed more at ease after talking to her, anyway.

She arrived at the docking section—industrial, full of struts and tubing, big external hatches lined up at intervals. The place was dusty; no matter how well ore and mineral cargo were secured in containers, dust inevitably accompanied mining operations. Made her nose itch whenever she came down here. The MilDiv ship was locking on and securing the hatch, able to do the work themselves without station-side crew. Made sense, with a ship whose main purpose seemed to be invasion. That left a dozen or so cargo crew personnel watching, pacing, their anxiety ramping up.

One of the docking chiefs spotted her. "What do we do? Do we resist? Should we try locking the doors?"

Lisle shrugged. Fighting would be valiant and useless. "This is above our pay grade. Let's just watch the show."

The control pad next to the hatch cycled through and lit green, and the steel mechanism of the hatch groaned open. Would a squadron of soldiers appear? Would they come out shooting and ask questions later? A couple of techs fled down the corridor, unwilling to risk whatever was about to come through the hatch. A couple of others glanced at Lisle to see what she was doing. She waited.

The hatch slid open, and two figures emerged. Just two. They really only needed two, dressed like that: in full streamlined armor that gleamed quicksilver gray under the docking bay lights, with close-fitting helmets and full-face visors. They looked inhuman, except for the way they moved, shifting to take up guard positions on either side of the hatch, scanning the gathered crew. They had guns, but the weapons remained holstered at their sides. Apparently, the crew outside was not a threat.

"Nobody be a hero, right?" Lisle murmured to her compatriots. "We don't get paid enough for this."

Someone chuckled darkly.

Some kind of consultation must have been happening via private comms. After a few moments of waiting—when no one in the docking bay seemed inclined to cause problems—a few more people emerged. No one else was wearing a full suit of armor, but Lisle had no doubt that they were all armed and capable of taking care of themselves.

A couple of bureaucratic types escorted by crew in militaristic uniforms left the *Visigoth* and went to other hatches, where shuttles to the planet were waiting for them. The auditing team, then. At this, some of the tension broke. Oddly, this was familiar—these people were just trying to do their jobs.

Meanwhile, the taller of the two figures in armor was coming toward her. She glanced around, and yes, she was the most senior Roth crew person here. At least, she had been before she'd resigned a half an hour ago. She stood her ground. Might have been smarter to get herself anywhere else. After the last couple of hours, she wasn't thinking that fast. She stood her ground and hoped she looked badass.

With the silvered-out faceplate, she couldn't see the soldier's eyes, but they clearly studied her, judging by the curious tilt to their head. Then the visor slid back into the helmet, revealing a roughly handsome man with a bit of stubble on a square jaw.

"You're Supervisor Rinzelli?" he asked.

Was she responsible, in other words? Was she a legitimate point of contact? She hoped not. "Uh. Yeah. Actually—no, I'm not, not anymore. I just resigned."

His expression broke into a ridiculously charming grin. Why did he need armor when he could just smile at everyone? This one was trouble, she just knew it.

"Wondered about that," he said. "We've been tracking your internal comms."

"Of course you have," she muttered. She shrugged, sheepish. In hindsight, sending the resignation felt childish, like a tantrum. Cowardly. "I just couldn't take it anymore."

"Understandable. I have to be honest, this job was a lot easier than we were expecting. We didn't think the code sabotaging the comms array would last more than an hour or two."

It wouldn't have, if she'd had her way. This was all just so . . . *typical.*

"I *knew* I should have gone out to do a manual reboot myself," she said, mostly to herself.

"You do that kind of thing?" the soldier asked, seeming genuinely curious. "Get your hands dirty?"

"Yeah, sometimes."

"Is all your work in navcom, or do you have more general systems management experience?"

After today, she was thinking she could make a go at Morganstern's job, if she wanted. This suddenly felt like more than general conversation. "Systems management would be the next step on my career path, I believe," she answered. "I think at this stage my options are wide open." *Come on, ask me about my strengths and weaknesses . . .*

"I'm Graff, by the way." He held out his gloved hand.

She took it reflexively and murmured, "Lisle. Hi."

"So," he said. "You looking for a job?"

Her breath caught. Was she? That meditative dream returned, floating in low-g in deep space, with a *competent* crew. Bliss.

"It's more of a quartermaster position," he went on. "Supply and organization, but we can always use someone with good problem-solving skills. And a little, you know . . . panache."

"Panache."

"That's right. So, what do you say?" His eyes *twinkled.* What sort of business did the *Visigoth* usually get up to? Well, she had today as a sample. But she had questions.

"Depends," she said cautiously.

"On what?"

"How many memos do you lot send on an average day?"

He scoffed. "Who has time for memos? We just use comms. So, you want to talk to the captain or not?"

"I would love to talk to your captain."

ABOUT THE AUTHOR ⎯⎯⎯⎯⎯⎯⎯⎯⎯⎯⎯⎯⎯

Carrie Vaughn's work includes the Philip K. Dick Award winning novel *Bannerless*, the New York Times Bestselling Kitty Norville urban fantasy series, over twenty novels and upwards of one hundred short stories, two of which have been finalists for the Hugo Award. Her latest novel, *The Naturalist Society,* is about 19th century ornithologists, awkward love triangles, and the magic of binomial nomenclature. An Air Force brat, she survived her nomadic childhood and managed to put down roots in Boulder, Colorado.

In Luck's Panoply Clad, I Stand
PHOEBE BARTON

Seven months since the war and two since winter should've ended, and Lake Erie is still frozen thick enough for me to walk out and gather care packages dropped from orbit. Soon enough, those metal husks will spill out harvests from Luna, Titan, Mirabilis; even worlds as far as Unserwald and Tamraparni are sending what they can spare.

Seven hungry months I waited before a ship warped in from La Mancha, full of mourning and grief. The messages didn't blame me for surviving where Hannelore and Zaynab hadn't. I wish they did. I do my best not to dwell on why.

It's easy to sink into those thoughts away from the shore. Out here, the water's deep enough that even I could drown in it. As I heft today's packages onto the sledge, the clouds part and Earth's sun delivers a dazzling haymaker. I'm left staggered for a moment despite my sunglasses. I can see so far, and too much of what I see is dead.

It's not easy being a giant after the end of the world, especially when the world isn't even yours.

"Of course you should go. The problem with this place is it's too damn small. Earth still has a billion years left."

I hadn't wanted to agree with my mother—it should've been a fight, her desire to keep me safe and close by against my need for distance and risk—but she could see it as clearly from her one and a half meters as I could from my six. La Mancha was a fragile winter garden, and I already felt huge enough to shatter it.

"You won't be alone, either. You, Zaynab, Hannelore . . . you're living proof of what humans can be when we break past our limits. I can't think of anyone I'd rather have represent our little world than you."

"They're so small on Earth. They're going to be afraid of me."

"Some people are afraid of everything. Give them a reason to be joyful instead."

It had been cold in Alturas Falls that day. I'd looked forward to feeling the heat of a new sun with Zaynab and Hannelore. They'd felt it for a microsecond when the sirens howled.

I still wonder if it would've been easier to have gone with them.

A snowfall picks up as I drag the sledge back to base, and I fall back on the satellites to guide me. The route leads me past dead trees, withered fields, and animals desperate in their innocence. The UN says enough missiles were intercepted that the cooling will be brief, but a green tomorrow is no relief for a world that's starving today.

My stomach rumbles to remind me that I'm part of that world now. On a good day, I'd eat as much as ten Earthers, and there haven't been any good days lately. I respond by quickening my pace; the base isn't far away now. The powered activity suit that lets me function in Earth's relentless gravity does most of the work, and electricity is one thing we have plenty of. The less food I get by with, the more is left for everyone else.

That all makes it easier to stumble. With the ground hidden beneath the snow, it's a rare mission that I don't lose my footing. I fall like I was taught, leaning into it and going slack, and my armor takes the pain. Without its power, I'd be crawling the rest of the way.

I see the flags first, flying above the gate. They're illuminated by spotlights that carve tunnels through the snow. The proud purple flag of my Haudenosaunee hosts waves next to the UN's galactic banner, and together they reinvigorate my resolve. This isn't the end of the world, only the end of one world and the beginning of another.

I wonder if being reminded of the galaxy's vast sweep, of so many worlds coming to their aid, makes Earthers feel comforted or merely small.

"Alice! I was wondering when you'd get back," Trillium Summer calls from the guard station. Xe was one of the first Earthers I'd met, back when my biggest responsibility had been representing La Mancha at the Galaxy Expo. "I seem to recall you being certain you'd beat the next snow."

"Yes, well, I'm still getting used to your funhouse of a planet." Xe steps out bundled thick against the cold and scans the packages as I watch for bandits. Thievery fell off sharply after those first terrible weeks, but there are always some who prefer food snatched from someone else's mouth.

"Keep your boots on the ground, and you'll do fine," Trillium says. "Though I don't know how you manage in that helmet. Your ears must be freezing."

"Self-preservation." A cracked head could kill an Earther born to this gravity, and they didn't have six meters to fall. After finishing with the packages, xe beckons me down, and I kneel.

"They said to keep it quiet, but you should know you've got a visitor," Trillium says. "Are you up to something?"

I stick out my tongue. "You think I'd leave you in the dark? For shame. Clearly, my reprehensible past has caught up with me."

I drag the sledge past the gate station and inside the walls of the UN Emergency Relief Agency's Niagara Hub. It had been assembled in a hurry and looked the part, but without the aid that had passed through here, a million more people would've starved to death by now. Halfway to the warehouse to get the packages checked in, someone with an ant's sense stands in my way.

"Can I help you?" I ask. Far more polite than *get out of the way, are you trying to get flattened?*

"Are you Alice Trimble?" As if it were possible to mix me up with anyone else. So far as I know, with Hannelore and Zaynab dead, I'm the only altan on Earth.

"That's me, and I'm busy." The warehouse isn't far, and I know they're waiting on me. "Can you clear a path?"

"Can I?" she says. "I'm Delphine Renault, MIP. I'm here to clear you a path home."

We were lucky the war wasn't even worse than it was. Not Zaynab and Hannelore, not the millions in Buffalo, Manaus, and the other pillars of salt that once were cities, but us. The survivors. It had been the middle of northern November, with the trees bare and the land already girded for a long, bracing dark, when a few death-loving presidents tried to murder Earth. A war in July would've shattered us all.

I knew I was lucky. The power plants, bridges, and people in Niagara Falls all should've made it an irresistible nuclear target. The attack sirens said as much, and long after their dirges ended, it took blood ebbing from my fists to convince me I hadn't died. I hated being lucky.

The first days were the hardest because while the nukes had spared us, the cruise missiles hadn't. Survivors dragged themselves in from Buffalo's shattered outskirts, soaked from black rain and desperate for more help than any of us could give. As I hefted supplies from surviving caches to half-wrecked hospitals, I saw people broken on cots, on blankets laid over the street, dying fast enough to see from the demolished logic of war.

I wasn't accustomed to high gravity then. A misstep that would have become a swift dance to regain my footing on La Mancha let the furious, mourning Earth suplex me. The flicker of terror I had time for reminded me that I wasn't dead, and my helmet's unyielding slam against the ground made sure of it.

When I yelled, it wasn't with surprise or pain. It was from the realization that it could have all ended right there, and how, in that moment, I would've been thankful if it had.

They'd fixed up what could've been a small warehouse for me to sleep and eat and piss in, seeing as how I can't fit in the barracks. It made a strange place to entertain a Member of Interstellar Parliament. She chooses to stand, and I make myself small, sitting and hugging my legs close. Not small enough, but I can never be small on Earth.

"They're keeping you like this? Beastly conditions."

I narrow my eyes at that. The place can get chilly, sure, but it's still walls, a roof, and the closest thing to home for fifty lightyears. Nairobi and Geneva had survived the war intact, and MIPs don't have to worry about their next meal while they snuggle in luxury.

"Things have been a bit difficult since the bombs," I say. "Maybe you've noticed."

"Yes, well, we're all doing our utmost to lift Earth up," Renault says. Probably because it's easier to think in platitudes than to think how many people are dying every day. "You're very much included in that, and no one doubts your commitment to the cause of reconstruction."

Even now, she's acting like she's running for office. No need to tell her she was at the bottom of my ballot. "Your tongue's polished enough, and I have work to do. Say your bit."

"As I said, I'm here to get you home."

Whenever the cold winds blow, which aren't rare in this winter that refuses to get off the stage, I'm reminded of home. La Mancha is a calm world, quiet, familiar—too familiar—and while on Earth I'm a curiosity, back there, I'm an experiment.

"It's been seven months. Did you not have time in your busy schedule before now?"

"The *Benengeli* only just came through the warp point," Renault says. "You've been doing good work, and we didn't see any reason to upset that balance. Now it's time for me to help you."

"The warp point's a month away," I say. "I don't intend to leave that soon."

"Ms. Trimble, there's assistance and then there's sacrifice. Certainly, Earth needs helpers, but it doesn't need everyone. La Mancha does. They've activated the Emergency Measures Act and declared duty to return."

I wince. The government must've panicked when news of the war reached them. Emergency measures meant curfews, checkpoints, and police in the streets, as if nukes would be falling on La Mancha next. That was bad enough, but nothing next to the arrogance of my government believing it had any right to order me home like a disobedient child.

"I never said I wasn't returning." Every morning, I groan from homesickness in my head and earthsickness in my bones. "But I won't push anyone out of the way to get there in a hurry."

"That's admirable, but your duty is—"

"Have you calculated how many people could be evacuated using the space I'd fill?" I unfold myself and stand up to my full six meters. My shadow roars across Renault like a nuclear echo. She doesn't flinch. "Because I have. What makes me more important than them?"

"I'm not talking about hypothetical people, but the very real person standing in front of me." She sits down on the cold floor, and her words hang. "Don't you think you matter at all?"

"Of course I matter." I take a step forward to really make the point. "Exactly as much as anyone else. I don't get extra votes because of how tall I am, so why is this different?"

"That power suit you're wearing should be all the answer you need," she says. "This isn't your world."

"If the Haudenosaunee or the LNAN ask me to leave, I'll listen." Earth had much more important things to worry about than whose hands were putting it back together. "By the way, I'm a bit behind on the news. How many refugees is La Mancha welcoming?"

"Ms. Trimble, you know how far we—"

"I figured as much." Last I heard, the exploration ships had made it as far as Bellatrix, five times farther out. "Try thinking about them before you think about me. Now, is that all? Like I said, I'm busy."

"Take some time to think about what I said," Renault says. "You have a place back home. You have important responsibilities—"

"Important?" I don't bother eating my laughter. "I signed off on reports and spreadsheets. Anyone could do that. Or is the Science Ministry desperate to see how the radiation's affected my precious engineered genes?"

"This is a crisis," Renault says after a moment, which gives me my answer. "This planet could see a flashover at any moment. Think about all the threats to La Mancha's survival if that happens. There are never enough hands. We need you, Alice."

I don't pay much attention to the news. Anything really important, I'd find out from people running or screaming or hearing explosions.

All I knew was that the Lunarian intervention put an end to the war before it could burn Earth down, and that Earth burning down wouldn't make La Mancha stop spinning. All Renault has are sunlight words, bright but massless.

I think about the stories I've heard from Mars, of how eager people are to leave those cracked and creaking domes, and of how cruelly exacting La Mancha's immigration requirements are: money, health, utility above all.

"People need me a lot more here at ground zero." I open the door, and the chill rolls in. It should remind her of home. "Thanks for stopping by."

I follow her out under a thick roof of steely clouds. As easy as it'd be to forget about the stars on days like this, it would be even easier to listen to my screeching bones and tell Renault I'd made a huge mistake.

I remind myself that running back home now isn't civic duty, but the worst kind of cowardice.

The war made New Year's Eve into a day of mourning with only the softest spice of hope, and however people expressed their hope, the true meaning was always "next year can't possibly be as bad, can it?" I spent it lying flat in my quarters, fully clothed but still naked, while technicians tried to figure out why my suit was broken.

"Should've brought a spare," one of the techs groused, as if it were easy to haul cargo across fifty lightyears, and ridiculous to expect anything from the largest, richest, most developed planet in the known galaxy. The only positive was that he wasn't afraid of me.

Not that he should've been, with me left prone, vulnerable, and absolutely useless.

"Don't be an ass, Samuel," said Cedric Li, director of the Niagara Hub and the man who'd helped me out of the rubble. His eyes were hidden behind a pair of incongruously celebratory 2278-shaped glasses. "The replacement suit gets here in November. All that matters for now is whether this one's fixable."

I'd been fortunate enough to survive not only the war, but high-gravity falls, aftermath diseases, and all the other methods Earth had to kill me. After hearing the news that they'd found a suit my size on Mars, I was ready to find that my reservoir of luck was empty. For Samuel to say it was a lost cause, and for me to steal the spots of twelve refugees as I was blasted into space, away from where I could make a difference.

"Not quickly," he said, which was both excellent and awful. Excellent because it was possible at all, and awful because until then I'd be at the mercy of the planet that invented rabies. I let myself stew in the sweat of it,

imagining all the people who'd starve because of me, until the technicians carried my suit away and Director Li kneeled next to my face.

"How can I help you, Alice?"

"You can't." Without my suit, I could clear debris about as well as a snake could sew. "All this fuss, and I can't even stand up. I'm useless."

"Don't lie to me, Alice." There was no anger there, only disappointment, and that was what surprised me. "There's more to recovery than lifting things. Do you have any idea how much paperwork this camp needs to process in just one day? There are never enough hands."

"You don't need me to do that," I said because I couldn't bring myself to say, "anyone could do that." If I ate as much as ten people, I had to do at least that much work, but without paperwork, the hub wouldn't have any supplies to deliver, and soon enough, nobody would be eating anything.

"Would you rather sacrifice what you can do because you're chasing after what you can't?" Li stared, and for an instant, I saw afterimages of mushroom clouds in his eyes. "I need what you can do, and we all need each other."

He may as well have been quoting La Mancha's constitution. Back home, society was a quilt, and everyone added patches in their own way.

"Okay," I said. "Okay."

After he left, I fought with the world. Two sit-ups that made all my muscles shriek at the indignity of being asked to work to their utmost were all I had in me that night.

It was a start.

The starship *Cide Hamete Benengeli* slid into orbit three days ago. I'd prefer to believe that the care package that La Mancha's embassy sent express to us, full of cryhawk eggs and Baie-Sereine wine and so many other flavors of home, was in recognition of all the work the Niagara Hub had done and not the supplies for a departure party, especially with the ambassador on his way.

I can't. Not when I'm about to be taken away.

"They said it's for *all* of us," Trillium says, lifting the slice of pie so much like an offering that it makes me shudder. We're alone in my temple-sized room. "Come on. This is special. Besides, they'll be here soon."

I'd hoped it was going to be a quiet night after my call with Renault. She'd begged me again to see reason and duty, and it had ended the same way as last time. After four weeks, Lake Erie's ice had receded, but people were still burning to get off Earth, and my principles were still solid.

"It's too much for me," I say, simultaneously a lie so transparent it made air look opaque and the utter truth. Every day I eat last, and the most awful stuff on offer: burned rice, chewy scum from the vats, and whatever scraps I can gather. They're enough. Anything more would feel like twisting off an Earther's limbs, sucking out the gristle and blood, and biting down on their head until sour brain erupts all over my tongue.

"Okay, but think about yourself once in a while, all right?" Trillium snaps the pie container's lid on with respectful solidity. "Otherwise, you'll lose yourself."

I'm already lost, and the smeared constellations tell me how unutterably far I've wandered. From Earth, Antares is flanked by a blazing retinue instead of a lone attendant, the stars of Félicette are shuffled between twin dippers, and the Young Rousseau is nowhere to be found. Only Orion is familiar, though squatter than I remember. A compass from home isn't worth anything here. It took Earth's survivors to point me in the right direction.

I don't tell Trillium any of this. I only say, "I'm fine," and it hangs for a moment before there's a knock on my door. I'd hoped the ambassador's helicopter would be late, but we're not far from what remains of New York.

"They'll be landing shortly," says Director Li. He doesn't bother trying to change my mind. He knows I've spent weeks forging my defiance into armor. "Are you ready?"

It would be so easy to say no. With one word, I could shrug off the leaden gravity of my principles. My legs are already trembling with the anticipation of weight.

"Yes," I say. "Let's go."

There's enough of a welcoming committee at the landing pad once we get there that I feel a twinge of guilt at all the work being left undone. I wrestle with my feelings until I hear an approaching helicopter's waspy buzz. Soon enough, it's on the ground, with its forward blades spinning at precisely the right height to slice my head off. I keep well back. The hub has enough responsibilities without having to clean up my corpse, too.

The ambassador alights after half a dozen operatives armed with electrolasers march out of the helicopter. Beneath his diplomatic finery, Charles Dupont is the color of raw chicken and hides his face behind the sickle curves of an imperial mustache.

"Ms. Trimble." He doesn't bother giving me a chance to speak first. "You've done well under exceptional circumstances."

"I have." I'm not about to accept praise from him. "Have you met Director Li? He can tell you stories."

"I'm afraid we don't have the time," Dupont says. "Alice Alcyone Trimble, in the name of Parliament, you are requested and required to return to La Mancha at the earliest opportunity."

"No." It's a complete sentence.

"That was not a question, Ms. Trimble," Dupont says as his operatives step toward me. "You are required—"

"Then make me." I motion to the drones buzzing above, mosquitoes next to the helicopter's bulk, and to all the hub staff watching us. "I'd like to remind you that kidnapping is a crime in the Haudenosaunee Confederacy."

Dupont hesitates as if he hadn't noticed the witnesses. "Be reasonable, Ms. Trimble. We're here to bring you home, in accordance with your civic duty."

"If you were reasonable, you'd be filling my space aboard *Benengeli* with twelve refugees," I say. "Even just to take them to Saturn. Are you? What about your duty to humanity?"

I pour all the frustration, anger, and grief of eight postwar months into my stare. Dupont doesn't flinch. Instead, he parries in exactly the way I expected.

"Your suit is property of the government of La Mancha," he says. "It is most assuredly coming with us."

"All right," I say. "You can have it."

I unfasten the suit's collar, shrug out of its sleeves, and let it fall. It lands with a solid enough thud that technicians back home would have cursed me and left me clad in an ordinary bodysuit that only protected from eyes. Nothing saves me from gravity now but my own wobbly legs.

Stepping away from the discarded suit takes everything I have. A misstep means a broken arm or leg at best. I keep my footing, and I stand defiant.

My body cries out, my sense of balance spins out of control, and my muscles go tense with terror. It's nothing I haven't practiced, and, if nothing else, I still have the security of my helmet. I'm clothed but naked and unafraid.

I stand.

"There you go," I say. "Is that it? Because we're busy."

Dupont scowls at me. All I can think of is how much everything hurts. Altan bones very literally weren't built for this, but to hell with it. Genetic engineers don't get to define my destiny, and neither does some windbag who's never slept on a hard floor or run supplies to a cutoff farmstead in the middle of a howling storm.

"This is your last chance," the ambassador says. "Let me remind you that the punishment for dereliction of duty to return is five years' imprisonment. Don't think they'll find you innocent when you come home."

My fists clench harder than my muscles. A few months on Earth radicalized me against revenge masquerading as justice, and that's all Dupont has. *Do what I say, or you'll be sorry.*

"Pass." My legs are quivering like toothpicks holding up a skyscraper now, but I won't let Dupont have the satisfaction of seeing me kneel. "I have work to do. Thanks for stopping by."

Director Li doesn't need to shout to send Dupont away without a prisoner. His everyday voice is an avalanche when necessary. My smile slides into a grimace as I round the corner behind the hangar, find a wall to lean against, and slide first to my knees, then my side. My breath goes raspy, and my heart is primed to explode. Maybe one day soon it will.

For now, it'll keep beating. It hasn't been a year since the war, and while I wait for my new Martian suit to cross the quiet emptiness, there's still a lot of work that I can do.

ABOUT THE AUTHOR

Phoebe Barton is a queer trans science fiction writer. Her short fiction has appeared in venues such as *Analog*, *Lightspeed*, and *Kaleidotrope*, and her story "The Mathematics of Fairyland" won the Aurora Award for Best Short Story in 2022. She lives with her family, nine typewriters, and many books in Hamilton, Ontario, Canada.

Space Bears and Engineering the Next Generation of Astronauts
GUNNAR DE WINTER

Tiny bears . . . in space!

In 2007, bears went to space for the first time. Poetically, they did so during the Russian Foton M3 mission.

These bears, however, weren't big, burly ursine cosmonauts, but microscopic animals known as tardigrades (aka water bears or, even cuter, moss piglets). Many of the over 1,500 tardigrade species live in the watery film on mosses or lichens. Some live among seaweed. As a group, tardigrades are biologically cosmopolitan, happily finding a home anywhere from the tropics to Antarctica.

Which leads us to our first clue on how to build better astronauts.

Our adorable slow walkers (the literal meaning of "tardigrade") have managed to establish themselves in almost every ecosystem because they are remarkably resilient.

Like big bears, our little bears can (kind of) hibernate. I included the "kind of" because tardigrades take it to the next level. They can enter a state of dormancy called cryptobiosis. During this phase, their metabolism drops to almost zero and, simultaneously, the water content in their body's tissues falls precipitously. Food? Water? No need. Tardigrade cryptobiosis can last for many (dozens of) years. For example, two water bears in a 1983 sample of frozen Antarctic moss were defrosted in 2016, and they happily went about their business as if nothing had happened.

Cryosleep and stasis are science fiction staples, and tardigrades have already figured out how to do it. How do our little friends do it, though? If they lose their internal water (a trick that prevents cellular damage by sharp frozen droplets), why don't they turn into raisins (bad idea for tissue integrity)?

Even compared to other animals that can handle extreme dehydration, tardigrades have a remarkable trick up one of their eight sleeves. With the help of one of the toughest tardigrade species, *Ramazzottius varieornatus,* researchers identified over 300 proteins that help our little bears bounce back after a dearth of water. Among these proteins, the scientists found plenty of so-called CAHS (cytoplasmic-abundant heat-soluble) proteins that were unique to tardigrades.

What these proteins do in the cells is turn the structural support (the cytoskeleton) into a firm gel. So, when tardigrades dehydrate, their tissues don't crumple or crack or become brittle. Instead, their cells turn into a kind of super-resilient Jell-O.

Turning into a blob doesn't sound appealing for human space explorers, however. Fortunately, tardigrades have more to offer.

Not a safe space

But wait. Why would human astronauts be interested in purloining biological skills from tardigrades?

While some organisms, like several microbes and tardigrades, can cope with at least a brief trip into space, Earth-based life simply hasn't evolved to deal with the vacuum of outer space. All life (as we know it) has evolved on a planet cuddled by an atmosphere. A rotating planet equals gravity, and an atmosphere equals protection against DNA-scrambling radiation blasts coming from space. Hence, our bodies tend to like the pull of gravity (in moderation, of course) and dislike exposure to excessive radiation (here too, it's the dose that makes the poison).

In contrast, space, that awe-inspiring void between the stars, is a realm with little gravity and lots of radiation. Space, unfortunately, isn't a safe place for humans.

Earth's atmosphere protects us from much of the radiation that travels through space. Without that atmospheric shield, our DNA would look like a four-letter alphabet soup. This means that to sail the sea of stars, we need protection. Even with all the physical barriers, drugs, and exercise regimes, long retreats into space—or merely to low Earth orbit, which isn't exactly deep space—are not good for human health.

And even flying to our neighboring planet, Mars, would take a while. If you get the timing right, it would take about nine months to get there, assuming current technology. That's a long time to be sleeping and eating and living in an active X-ray machine . . . (A chest X-ray is roughly 0.1 milliSievert [mSv], and the average astronaut is exposed to 300 mSv on the International Space Station [ISS] in a year.)

Yet, putting boots on extraterrestrial ground has always allured us, but to contemplate this, it is time for a radiation exposure cost-benefit analysis for our next trip to Mars.

Luckily, a 2021 study did such an analysis.

To start, consider two major and dangerous types of radiation—solar energetic particles and galactic cosmic rays. Next, subtract what current shielding options can mitigate. Then, calculate the maximum duration for a Mars mission (flights and potential stay included) that would keep radiation exposure under 1,000 mSv. (Sidenote: NASA has recently revised its lifetime exposure limit for astronauts to 600 mSv.)

With that in mind, how long does our (one-way or round, your choice) Mars trip last if we want to stay within the "baked but not burned" overall radiation exposure level? Four years or less.

Tricky but doable, especially when you consider that researchers are developing new materials that combine a relatively light weight with better shielding properties, such as hydrogen-rich composites. As we develop better technology and materials, the overall radiation exposure of our missions to Mars (and beyond) will go down. And that's only one of the things we can do.

How about building biological shields?

What's Dsup?

Beyond their remarkable cryptobiosis ability, our tiny tardigrades carry their own radiation shield, almost as if evolution randomly cobbled together little proto-astronauts.

More specifically, our friendly water bears have molecular armor in the form of the unique protein Dsup. Dsup (the cool name for "damage suppressor") is a DNA protector protein. Radiation that would shred every picogram of DNA in any other animal? A little Dsup and the tardigrades are all right.

We can take the DNA armor metaphor literally. Recently, Dsup was identified as an intrinsically disordered protein. It has no fixed 3D structure, which allows it to flexibly alter its shape so that it matches that of the DNA it needs to protect.

Here's the kicker for human astronauts: a preprint suggests that human cells can incorporate Dsup and use it to become more radiation resistant. Research in mice even shows how Dsup can protect healthy tissue during radiation therapy for cancer.

Of course, cells in a petri dish and lab mice are far from complex human bodies, and we won't become happily spacefaring creatures anytime soon. But can we fiddle with our biology to mitigate some of the more detrimental aspects of space exploration? Could we possibly use the latest gene-editing technology, the growing coterie of CRISPR versions, to boost our biology?

CRISPR, or Clustered Regularly Interspaced Short Palindromic Repeats, is the name for DNA sequences that were first identified in bacteria in 1987. Let's translate that mouthful of CRISPR's full name: these DNA sequences are short, clustered together, the same if you read them from front to back or back to front (palindromic), repeated, and regularly interrupted by other DNA chunks.

At the time of their discovery, these sequences were considered a bacterial oddity. A niche interest. It took twenty years before scientists figured out that CRISPR sequences protect bacteria against repeated viral infections. CRISPR allows bacteria to integrate bits of virus DNA into their genome, which helps them quickly recognize another infection by the same virus and cut the invader's genome into pieces before it can do much harm. Then, in 2012, the Nobel-worthy breakthrough came. Jennifer Doudna, Emmanuelle Charpentier, and their colleagues, as well as Feng Zhang and his team, developed gene-editing tools based on CRISPR and the DNA-cutting protein Cas9. CRISPR-Cas was born, and it brought gene editing to the scientific masses, so to speak.

In the past decade, CRISPR has blossomed into a wide array of tools that use different DNA-snipping proteins. We now have CRISPR systems that can precisely edit a single DNA letter without having to snip the double helix (base editors) or target RNA or the epigenome instead of the DNA itself.

In short, CRISPR is a gene-editing system that lets scientists target and alter specific DNA (or RNA) sequences. Combine CRISPR with the fact that some earthly beasts have genetically encoded superpowers like Dsup we might borrow, and it's time to "build" the next generation of astronauts.

Enhanced astronauts

Radiation is arguably the greatest (but far from the only) health challenge of spaceflight. Introducing the earlier-mentioned Dsup into astronaut genomes might improve cellular resilience against the ionizing radiation that pervades space beyond our cuddly atmosphere. We can go even smaller and look at the bacterium *Deinococcus radiodurans*, one of the most radiation-resistant organisms ever known. *D. radiodurans* was discovered in the 1950s, when scientists wanted to try preserving food by bombarding meat with levels of gamma radiation that killed all known forms of life. After being showered by 3,000 times the level of radiation that would kill a human, the meat still spoiled. *Deinococcus* was hungry, and radiation couldn't stop the bacterium. Its genome contains multiple DNA repair pathways and antioxidant systems. We could pick and choose the best ones (such as manganese-based antioxidants or enhanced homologous recombination repair genes) to give our next-gen astronauts even better internal radiation shields.

But let's say some radiation gets through, as it inevitably will. In that case, we can go big. For example, large animals like elephants and whales get less cancer than we'd expect given their body size (which correlates with the number of cells and so more cells than can go cancerous over a lifetime). This decoupling of cancer rate and cell number is known as Peto's paradox. So, how do our big mammal cousins do it? There are a few mechanisms, but the most straightforward one involves a gene called *TP53,* also known as the guardian of the genome. In short, the protein encoded by this gene, p53, prevents mutations.

In fifty percent of human cancers, something goes wrong with *TP53*. What's the elephant trick? Well, humans have one copy of the *TP53* gene. Elephants have twenty (mammoths had fourteen). Adding a few extra *TP53*s to the astronaut genome might just help guard their genomes.

Earth has its protective atmosphere thanks to gravity, but gravity does more than keep our radiation shield in place. The gravitational force that shaped both Newton's and Einstein's careers has also shaped the evolution of our bodies. Our bones and muscles *need* gravity. Take it away, and muscles atrophy and bones demineralize. Here, super-cows might come to the rescue. The Belgian Blue cattle breed (aka *dikbil* or "fat butt" in Dutch) is known for its remarkably muscular appearance. Their lean, hyper-muscular physique is the result of a single mutation in the gene for myostatin, which acts as a brake on muscle development. Take away the brake, and . . . ta-da, Hercules cow. This is not unknown in humans *and* mice that visited the ISS while being treated with myostatin blockers kept their muscle and bone mass, suggesting that silencing or editing the myostatin gene in astronauts could reduce atrophy during long missions.

We could even add some (non-tardigrade) bear genes to our astronauts. Bears that hibernate don't lose bone density like humans in space or on bed rest do. This is less convenient to mimic because it involves 5,000 genes, but the pathways of bone remodeling might be amenable to a little tweak here and there in astronauts.

Okay, our astronauts can deal with radiation and safeguard their DNA, as well as stay strong in bone and muscle. So far, so good. What about microbes? Bacterial and viral infections? Spaceflight, after all, dysregulates the immune system and can lead to the activation of latent viruses, waiting for a moment of weakness. Of course, we can (partially) address this with supplements and medications. We can also look at a few interesting rodents.

For example, naked mole rats possess a resilient immune system that maintains strong innate defenses while avoiding chronic inflammation. Their tissues produce—deep breath—high-molecular-weight hyaluronan, which suppresses cancer development, dampens unnecessary inflammation, and helps the mucus barrier in the nose and lungs resist respiratory and gastrointestinal infections. Naked mole rats also show enhanced responses to viral threats. When it comes to viruses, however, it's hard to beat bats. Bats tolerate high viral loads without triggering harmful inflammation. How do they do it? Our winged friends have type I interferons (proteins that signal the body to fight viruses) that are active all the time. Their immune system is scanning for threats 24/7. Not only that, but they have sensitive versions of virus-detecting proteins like MDA5 and PKR, which help them recognize and control viruses very efficiently. Finally, when dealing with an infection, the bat immune system dials down something ominously called the NLRP3 inflammasome, which normally triggers strong inflammatory responses. This helps chiropterans avoid tissue damage and stay healthy, even when dealing with an infection.

As humanity inches closer to long-duration space missions, astronauts will increasingly face a host of physiological and environmental stressors, including high-energy radiation, muscle and bone atrophy, and immune dysregulation, to name only a few. Nature offers a wild bestiary of genetic adaptations to extreme environments, from radiation-proof tardigrades to cancer-resistant elephants. With advances in CRISPR and gene therapy, we can now at least entertain the notion of enhancing astronauts to be more capable of dealing with space travel.

Such enhancements are, for now, ethically complex and technically challenging. "Could" never implies "should." However, at the tail end of 2023, the FDA approved the first CRISPR-based therapy (CASGEVY™)

for beta thalassemia and sickle cell disease, with dozens of successfully treated patients so far. Similar therapies are in the works for cystic fibrosis and other conditions. Earlier this year, an infant with a rare metabolic disease received a personalized CRISPR therapy. The little boy, KJ, is growing and thriving.

Gene editing is here. Incipient, tentative, and in need of more research, yes.

A DNA shield sounds good, though.

ABOUT THE AUTHOR

Gunnar De Winter is a Belgian biologist-turned-science writer who has studied bacteria wars, hustling hermit crabs, social spiders, running lizards, and human/robot behavior. His stories have appeared in, among others, *Heartlines Spec, The Deadlands,* and *Future SF Digest.*

Memory, Loss, and Memory Loss:
A Conversation with Rich Larson

ARLEY SORG

Rich Larson was born in Galmi. Even as a small child in Niger—before he could write—he would tell his sisters stories; or sometimes, he would tell stories to himself. Years later, while in Canada, he was inspired to keep writing by a short story contest held at a local library. Larson studied French and Spanish in university and took a poetry class as well as a playwriting class. At nineteen, he spent a year studying creative writing in Providence, Rhode Island and published a number of literary (nonspeculative) poems and short stories, all of which led to a sense of disenchantment. The ensuing summer, his unpublished cyberpunk thriller *Devolution* was a finalist for an Amazon Breakthrough Novel Award, which further inspired him to spend his energy writing in the speculative field. Shortly after, he self-published speculative collection *Datafall*. Around that time, his work began appearing in speculative venues, including "Last" in *Daily Science Fiction* in September 2012,

141

"Let's Take This Viral" in *Lightspeed* in March 2013, and "The Mermaid Caper" in *Beneath Ceaseless Skies* in April 2013.

Larson attended Clarion West in 2014, though his career in short fiction was already well underway, arguably demonstrated by winning the 2014 Dell Magazines Award for Undergraduate Excellence in Science Fiction and Fantasy for "The Nostalgia Calculator," plus his twenty or so publishing credits—many of them at pro-rate venues. He moved to Spain and then went back to Canada, to Edmonton, Alberta, and then moved again to Ottawa. During that period, he published a slew of short fiction and had multiple appearances in various Year's Best anthologies. Larson was working toward a translation certificate when he landed his first book deal. "The advance let me abandon my studies and my job at the liquor store, and I've been writing full-time ever since." Orbit published debut novel *Annex* in 2018, which was a Locus Award finalist. Talos published the collection *Tomorrow Factory* later that year. Not long after this, Larson moved to Prague.

Rich Larson has well over two hundred short stories out and several collections, plus longer works, including the aforementioned *Annex*, and 2022 Orbit novel *Ymir*. He has been nominated for three Sunburst Awards, was a Philip K. Dick finalist for *Ymir*, and won a Eugie Award for "Quandary Aminu vs The Butterfly Man" (Tor.com September 2022).

"I've been lucky enough to live in a few great places and pass through many others, but I'm trying to settle down in Montreal. I recently hit the three-year mark here, which is my longest stay in one city since high school." Not one to feel complacent, Larson attended Sycamore Hill in 2024. When he's not writing, he's still pushing himself creatively: "Lately I'm really into life drawing, pool, and soulless corporate yoga. I'm trying to do a ten-second handstand before the year is out; my record so far is eight."

Rich Larson's recent collection is *Changelog*, released last month by Fairwood Press; he also rereleased his self-illustrated flash collection *The Sky Didn't Load Today and Other Glitches* in August.

Who do you see as some of your literary heroes, or what are some of the works you see as important to or inspirational for you, and why?

I was recently back in Grande Prairie, and found this cluster of childhood favorites at my parents' house:

All these authors shaped how I write. Thanks to Megan Whalen Turner, any acerbic underdog I create will have shades of Eugenides—and just months ago, I polished off a fantasy novelette full of Queen's Thief-esque political maneuvering. Cornelia Funke had a big influence on my YA debut, *Annex*, and there are bloody echoes of William Nicholson's Wind on Fire trilogy in my novel, *Ymir*.

Graham Gardner's *Inventing Elliot* and C. S. Lewis's *Till We Have Faces* were both revelatory to me as a kid. The protagonist of my gory *Clarkesworld* story "Extraction Request" took his name from the former; the title of my even gorier *Apex* story "You Too Shall Be Psyche" came from the latter.

Kenneth Oppel (who also wrote *Dead Water Zone, Silverwing*, and a slew of more recent, likely equally excellent stuff) is the guy who proved to me, via a brief phone call when I was six, that books are written by real people. I had the audacity to look him up decades later and ask him to blurb *Ymir*; he very politely declined and added that blurbs rarely affect sales, which we all know in the back of our minds, but damn, I love blurbs. My *Lightspeed* flash "To Navigate the Night" is basically *Silverwing* fanfic.

My single greatest influence is likely M.T. Anderson's *Feed*. It's a master class in neologisms—right from the jump, readers are hit with an avalanche of invented slang that makes perfect sense from context. It's also a scalpel-sharp exploration of class, consumerism, and late capitalism, plus a tear-jerking tragedy with messy, incredibly human characters. Pretty much everything I write has some *Feed* in its DNA.

You've been publishing short fiction for over a decade now. How did you first get into writing, and at what point did you decide to take writing seriously?

I've been writing stories for most of my life, and before that, I told them to my older sisters and asked them to transcribe. As a kid, I entered a short story contest at the local library every year and won it consistently until my stories got too gross/violent/depressing for the judges. I started selling to magazines not long after high school—but it was my first book deal, in 2018, that gave me the financial cushion to go full-time.

My novels have yet to earn out, but I make a nonglamorous living via sporadic work-for-hire projects, steady short fiction sales, and the occasional film option, all supplemented by royalty trickles and Patreon subscribers.

(You could be one of them! I feel weird about that exclamation mark, but I'm doubling down!)

How has your writing or your writing process changed after over a decade in publishing and a massive amount of written words committed to a slew of narratives?

The quality has definitely improved; the process, debatable. I still spend a lot of time banging my head against plot-walls and starting stories that go nowhere. The key difference is that I'm less anxious riding out the lulls and blank page days. That's the biggest gift experience has granted me: accumulated evidence that things will eventually untangle themselves and the words will start flowing again.

You are probably among the most prolific short fiction writers working in SFF today. Thinking about your body of work, what are one or two you would most want people to look at?

I'd steer them toward two *Changelog* novelettes that are also available online: biopunk thriller "Quandary Aminu vs The Butterfly Man," which won the 2023 Eugie Foster Memorial Award, and slow-burn novelette "You Are Born Exploding," which was published right here in *Clarkesworld* and later translated into Polish and Chinese—also, Rich Horton loved it, and that guy has good taste.

These two stories are diametrically opposed in pace and vibe, and they're two of the best things I've ever written.

Orbit published novels Annex and Ymir. Do you find the novel-writing process more challenging in certain ways than short fiction?

I have a love-hatehatehate relationship with novels. Planning doesn't come easily to me, and revising a novel is a lot more work than revising a short story. That said, I do have something bubbling on the mental back burner. Maybe I'll get to it in 2026.

You have had work translated into visual formats, including animated shows Love, Death & Robots and Secret Level, for which you have a teleplay credit as well. What are some of your most important observations or thoughts on stories transformed into visual media?

When many cooks are in the kitchen, you have to learn to let go of the whisk. Yes, it's all kitchen metaphors from here on out.

I love the Netflix adaptation of "Ice," particularly Robert Valley's incredibly kinetic art style, but it's quite distinct from the short story—for one thing, it has a happy ending. Similarly, the work I did for *Secret Level* evolved on its way to screen. As much as I enjoy the opportunity to play in other people's IP, I have to slot this kind of work-for-hire writing into a different part of my brain. Otherwise, the diminished creative control would get to me.

Are there concerns or themes that you often come back to in your work, or do you see your work as varying too much to definitively discuss a set of primary concerns?

Everybody has their shit, as my mom told me one wine-slick Christmas. Historically, that's been fraught sibling relationships; lately, I'm into memory, loss, and memory loss. But those stories still represent a small fraction of the corpus, and I'm always searching for new angles and material, new ways to stretch myself in order to not get bored/boring.

In the past couple years, that meant cowriting experiments and a foray into novellas. This year, I'm trying to write ten sequels (or prequels) to previously published stories; I have an aversion to double-dipping with characters or settings, so it's been a challenge.

If you've read a story of mine you believe is in dire need of a follow-up, feel free to get in touch.

Changelog is your fourth collection. When you think of your earlier collections, Datafall, Tomorrow Factory, and The Sky Didn't Load Today, what sets this book apart for you?

Changelog had a much, much longer gestation period. *Datafall* was a self-pub experiment when I was twenty; *The Sky Didn't Load Today and Other Glitches* is flash-only, illustrated, small press.

Changelog, though, is the full-size follow-up to my 2018 collection *Tomorrow Factory*—a book that exceeded my wildest expectations. It earned out against the advance; its French counterpart, *La Fabrique des lendemains*, won the Grand Prix de L'Imaginaire, and a couple of the stories within netted film/TV options.

I figured a second collection would follow quickly, but due to the vagaries of publishing, it took seven years. Because I spent that entire time writing new stories, *Changelog*'s table of contents saw many iterations—and the long wait did the book good.

It let me put a lot of thought into the structure: varying lengths, themes, and tones, seeking out natural clusters and pauses for breath. I was able to polish up the prose of older stories, iron out the occasional inconsistency, and take my time adding behind-the-scenes author notes plus a full bibliography.

What do you see as the role of collections for authors as well as for publishing—what makes them important?

The publishing landscape is in rapid flux, and I know almost nothing about it, so I'll just take the personal angle. For me, assembling and curating a collection brings a lot of creative joy—and also gets me nostalgic as hell because the individual stories are like little time capsules.

Rereading them reminds me where I was, who I was, who I was with when I wrote them. When drifting lonely as a cloud through a fairly confusing existence, it's nice to have anchor points like that.

Most of the stories in Changelog were published within the past seven years or so, but the earliest publication date is "Like Any Other Star," originally published in AE: The Canadian Science Fiction Review. What is interesting about this piece, what made it a story that you wanted new readers to see?

That was my very first pro sale, so part of my motivation was the time capsule thing described above. My reread took me back to age nineteen, recently emboldened by my success with the Amazon Breakthrough Novel Award, back before Amazon was the devil, when the idea of writing for a living was just starting to percolate.

But it's also just a solid little story not radically different from one I'd write now, which is sort of terrifying—have I grown at all as a writer? Have I changed at all as a person? These are the questions I like to dash myself against. Sometimes it seems like a binary switch utterly dependent on how much serotonin I have swirling around in my brain.

Fun fact: ten years and two hundred sales after this publication, the editor who bought it for *AE* stumbled across "LOL, Said the Scorpion" here in *Clarkesworld*, recognized my name, and saw from my bio that we'd both ended up in Montreal. Now we write together once a week and often play pool at a particular dive bar.

The most recent offerings are "Headhunting" (Tor.com 2023), "Quandary Aminu vs The Butterfly Man" (Tor.com 2022), and "Dale Dale Dale" (Martian: The Magazine of Science Fiction Drabbles 2022). What can you tell readers about these stories without "spoiling" the read too much?

"Headhunting" was the final addition to the ToC, and I'm very glad it made the cut: it's a grimy bouncy detective story (casefic?) in which a hallucinating PI is hired to track down a mummified head stolen from a cathedral. The scene where he saws a lime green cast off his arm with a steak knife is pulled directly from my own life. It took forever.

I go through phases when it comes to story length, and I was on a huge drabble kick when I wrote "Dale Dale Dale." Very easy to spoil, so I'll just say it's body horror inspired by an ancient Xbox game and a Jaime Sabines poem.

I've already touched on "Quandary Aminu vs The Butterfly Man," but I'll drop a quote from Ted Kosmatka, *Portal 2* writer and author of *The Flicker Men*: "There's a reason Larson's vivid, driven stories end up as these great animated short films. And I think I've just read the next one. 'Butterfly Man' is begging for an animated adaptation."

You just rereleased your earlier collection, The Sky Didn't Load Today and Other Glitches, which features some of your illustrations. What would you like readers to know about that book?

If you're undecided on *Changelog*, grab *The Sky Didn't Load Today and Other Glitches* first. It's a smaller time/cash commitment, gives a good idea of my tonal range, and features little brush pen illustrations—an exciting first for me.

Montreal is lousy with visual artists, and moving here triggered a tiny personal renaissance: I've been life drawing twice a week, doing *plein air* in various parks, and taking a charcoal portrait class. Stuff like this:

When this flash collection first started coming together, I floated the idea of internal illustrations—and the original publisher, Eric Fomley, told me to run with it. That kicked off a summer of sketching, reworking, polishing, and eventually finishing thirty small black-and-white pen drawings. Like so:

 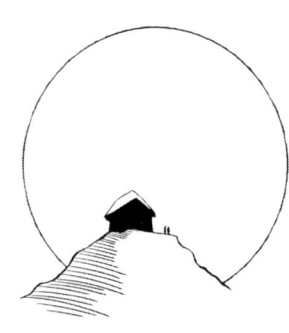

It would not have been possible without a bunch of wonderful, highly skilled artist friends who offered feedback, advice, and encouragement throughout.

Is there anything else you'd like Clarkesworld readers to know about you, your work, or Changelog?

If you, *Clarkesworld* reader, have made it to the bottom of this incredibly long interview—you already know more about me, my work, and *Changelog* than pretty much anyone on Earth. You have done enough. I salute you.

ABOUT THE AUTHOR

Arley Sorg is an associate agent at kt literary. He is a two-time World Fantasy Award Finalist and a two-time Locus Award Finalist for his work as co-Editor-in-Chief at *Fantasy Magazine*. Arley is also a SFWA Solstice Award Recipient, a Space Cowboy Award Recipient, and a finalist for two Ignyte Awards. Arley is senior editor at *Locus*, associate editor at both *Lightspeed* & *Nightmare*, a columnist for *The Magazine of Fantasy and Science Fiction* and an interviewer for *Clarkesworld*.

Technology as a Language:
A Conversation with Ken Liu

ARLEY SORG

If you read *Clarkesworld*, or for that matter, any of the major science fiction and fantasy magazines, you've probably heard of Ken Liu. In our 2020 *Clarkesworld* interview, we noted that he had "100+ short stories, novelettes, and novellas," and of course, being a prolific creative, he has continued to publish high-quality work since then. His fiction is often described as thought-provoking or even heartbreaking.

Ken Liu was born in China and grew up in the US. He went to Harvard, concentrating in English and computer science, including taking several creative writing classes. He also earned his JD at Harvard. He worked in technology for several years, including time at Microsoft as an engineer and at a startup in Cambridge, and he practiced law for a number of years, including working as a litigation consultant. Along the way, he was an active member of online writing workshops and organizations.

Liu began publishing with 2002 story "Carthaginian Rose" but really hit his stride around 2011, by which time his work had garnered significant acclaim. He had a slew of stories come out that year, and he started landing on awards lists, including "The Paper Menagerie" (*The Magazine of Fantasy and Science Fiction* March-April 2011), which was a finalist for both Locus and Sturgeon awards, and won Nebula, World Fantasy, and Hugo awards—plus a couple more awards after being translated. Liu's debut novel, *The Grace of Kings*, came out in 2015 with Saga Press and was a Nebula finalist as well as a Locus Award winner. That book started his series The Dandelion Dynasty. Collection *The Paper Menagerie and Other Stories* came out in 2016 with Saga and was a World Fantasy finalist as well as a Locus Award winner. Shortly after publication, Liu went full-time as a writer in 2017. Collection *The Hidden Girl and Other Stories* came out from Saga in 2020 and was, again, a Locus Award winner. To date, Liu has been up for, and often won, most of the major SFF awards, some of them multiple times, including being a Nebula Award finalist nine times and taking three Hugo Awards wins.

Liu's official bio will tell you that he "frequently speaks at conferences and universities on a variety of topics, including futurism, cryptocurrency, history of technology, bookmaking, the mathematics of origami, and other subjects of his expertise." In his own words: "I'm a futurist and have done work with the UN, government think tanks, and the World Economic Forum. I spend a not insignificant amount of time consulting with tech companies and attending tech/science conferences." On a personal note, I have interviewed him at least four times now, and I always find he has unique and interesting perspectives; each conversation presents something new, something deeply fascinating.

Ken Liu lives near Boston, MA with his family. *All That We See or Seem*, the first entry in a near-future thriller series, is due this month from Saga Press. A collection tentatively titled *The Passing of the Dragon and Other Stories* is scheduled for publication in 2026.

Did the pandemic and global lockdown change anything about your writing or your career? Is your writing practice more or less back to how it was before lockdown?

The pandemic itself forced me to reckon with the value and aim of storytelling in general. My general optimism in the power of storytelling for good was challenged by the prevalence of harmful conspiracy narratives—acts of collective storytelling—that are now one of the sobering lessons of the pandemic. I paused for a time and reexamined why stories matter. Seeking solace in words and ideas that have endured past tumults, I began a deep engagement with the *Dao De Jing*, which has changed my outlook.

My reflection on the value of storytelling and conversation with the Dao became the spine of *All That We See or Seem*.

You've been in the writing game for a while now. What has surprised you about the publishing industry, what has disappointed you, and what have been the best things?

The business of books continues to surprise me by the degree to which it's not "businesslike." It's an industry where an idiosyncratic love of books still shapes decisions—a feature that makes some things messier and many things more meaningful. I like working with people who fundamentally believe that books are valuable not just as objects to be sold, but as artifacts that deserve to be created and shared in themselves.

Attention is more fragmented than ever, and that makes discovery even more challenging. But the desire for good stories has not waned. The fact that I've been able to do something that brings me a great deal of joy and make a living from it is incredible. I'm thankful every day.

Many describe science fiction as an ongoing conversation, and there are some authors who write works that are in deliberate dialogue with other works. Do you feel that All That We See or Seem is in dialogue or conversation with any particular works?

I'll start with a quick logline for the novel to give some context: Julia Z, a reclusive hacker, is asked to rescue an AI-aided dream-artist from an international crime ring. But as she travels across the country, hunting and being hunted, she realizes that she must confront the darkness in her own past and in her psyche.

All That We See or Seem is certainly in conversation with *Do Androids Dream of Electric Sheep?* (more so than with its film adaptation, *Blade Runner*). Both explicitly engage with the role of dreaming in a hyper-rationalist, hyper-technological society. The dream artist in my novel, Elli, is a conscious response to Mercer, the prophet of Mercerism.

Dreaming was, for much of human history, a fundamental mode of knowing, but in the post-Freudian age, it's been relegated to the realm of nonsense, of mere brain "noise." In fact, the rise of attention-soaking technologies like doomscrolling and short-form video has even eliminated the cousin of dreaming, daydreaming, by displacing boredom.

But dreaming is when we travel into the collective unconscious, where we find, paraphrasing Le Guin, myth, spirituality, gods, and monsters. When we cease to dream, we cease to be human.

Both *Do Androids Dream of Electric Sheep?* and *All That We See or Seem* are about the forms dreaming can take when technology is used to reshape consciousness, when we are forced to define what it means to be human in a world where machines become ever more humanlike.

Likewise, as indicated by the reference to Le Guin above, my book is certainly also in conversation with her works, which deal extensively with our engagement with the mythic in dreams.

Is dream technology, as a science-fictional concept, similar to supernatural or magical ideations of dream interactions and manipulation, or are there important differences? Are there things about the approach in All That We See or Seem that arise from your background as a technologist, or that relate more directly to science?

I view technology largely as a manifestation of human nature, rather than something alien to it. Technology—machines, software, systems—consists of patterns in the mind made tangible. Therefore, my approach is to examine how technology, like language itself, both expresses and transforms our humanity. The collective-dreaming technology in *All That We See or Seem* offers an alternative to the conspiratorial narratives shaping our politics today. Still, both share the same root in our hunger for meaning and a sense of belonging.

What made you want to write a thriller, and did writing a thriller mean learning or developing new sets of writing skills?

I've always enjoyed reading thrillers. I admire the way everything—characterization, worldbuilding, backstory—has to be delivered "on the fly." You're always on the run, and there's never enough time to get the "whole story." It's the total opposite of the way I like to tell a story.

I figured it was time to try to do one myself. But when it comes to writing, I've never been someone to take the conventions of a genre as they are. Whatever I end up writing, it's always unmistakably me. *All That We See or Seem* is no different.

It's a propulsive near-future thriller (break-ins, chases, moral choices under surveillance) with a focus on relationships (found family tied together through memory, shared stories, and second chances). But it's also entwined with meditative episodes on dreaming as a shared medium: What dreams do we share as Americans? Who gets to shape the dream of the republic?

Are there challenges to writing near-future science fiction that are very different from far-future science fiction?

I've heard the view that near-future SF is hard because you risk becoming outdated very quickly (publishing moves slowly, while technology changes fast). I don't worry about that very much. Even when I'm writing near-future SF, I'm really mining for the mythology of technology. In that sense, what I'm writing is realism, not speculation.

Who is Julia Z, how do you describe her, and what do you find most compelling about her?

Julia Z is a hacker, someone who enjoys studying machines and systems and working out how to get them to do what she wants. She's particularly skilled at working with AI. After a horrific childhood, she found a home among a group of hackers and then got involved in cybercrimes, for which she was punished. She's now trying to pick up the pieces and just live a "normal" life.

But, as is the nature of these things, fate finds a way to yank her back into trouble, and she must use her unique set of skills to save those she loves, and perhaps the world, too.

I first met Julia Z in the aftermath of the pandemic. One day, as I was thinking about the consequences of ubiquitous AI on the arts, she simply appeared and told me that I was wrong. The real danger of AI, she told me, had nothing to do with the Singularity or the displacement of humans by machines; instead, it was the way we would all start to treat each other as machines. I found that intriguing and wanted her to tell me more. That was how I came to know her.

What was the inspiration behind Elli, and what is important to know about her?

I think a lot about what it means to be an artist in the age of AI.

I'm not terribly concerned about machines displacing human artists—this is limited to a specific conception of what "artist" means—because I don't believe mere imitation of what humans do by machines is all that interesting. Note that I'm not saying that imitation of humans by machines wouldn't be *profitable*, but fundamentally, I don't want to conflate the business of art with the practice of art itself.

I am excited, however, by the possibility of new forms of art that could be enabled by human artists using AI. The analogy here would be cinema. After the invention of the motion picture camera, merely pointing it at a stage play and replaying the film was not interesting. It wasn't until artists figured out how motion pictures represented a new medium and devised the language of cinema, telling stories in a way that was impossible in the absence of the machine, that the full potential of the motion-capturing machine was revealed. The full potential of AI as its own artistic medium, likewise, will not be clear until human artists figure out what to do with it (and that is certainly not using it to create cheap copies of things human artists already do).

Elli is one of these artists. As a pioneer, an oneirofex, she uses AI as a way to help people dream together. That's her art. It brings people together. But like any artist, what she does is also dangerous and gets her in trouble. That's where Julia comes in.

What is your approach to writing or utilizing science-fictional concepts in general, and how does your approach in All That We See or Seem compare with what you usually do?

While I do enjoy the technical details of technology, in terms of my fiction, I'm usually focused on technology as a language, a way for humans to express themselves. This means I'm interested in how inventors, users, hackers, salespeople, critics, scammers, and everyone else express who they are through what they do with my fictional technology. You could say that's my trademark: treating technology as a language. *All That We See or Seem* is no different.

What do you most want readers to know about All That We See or Seem, what is central or important about this story?

This is not a story that portrays an AI-filled future as either utopian or dystopian. I don't find either particularly interesting. As I said before, this is a realist story that focuses on how humans express themselves through the language of technology—and, specifically, how they dream in the age of AI.

What do you see as the relationship between technology and art, and what do you see as the evolution of that relationship across the next decade or so?

It's really the core question for the Julia Z series.

While the details will be unpredictable, I think some large patterns are clear. Like all aspects of life, art is very much driven by technology now and will become increasingly so in the future. Our most popular and influential art forms—cinema, short-form video, memes—are all heavily mediated by technology and are impossible without technology. I think the anxieties over AI and art are real, but in the long term, artists will figure out what to do with AI, and we'll be all the richer for it.

Thinking about your prodigious body of work, what does *All That We See or Seem* say about your evolution as a writer, and what are the ways that you hope to challenge yourself in the future?

If there's one thing that I hope is true about myself as an artist, it's that over time, I've grown to care less and less about the general opinion. To make art that is true to your vision, to your journey through life and the collective unconscious, you must be willing to be disliked—when you tell stories that are not cliches, you make some people uncomfortable. This doesn't mean you deliberately make things that you think will be disliked—just that a people-pleasing attitude is anathema to art.

I feel that *All That We See or Seem* gets closer to my vision of authentic art. I'm proud of that.

Is there anything else you'd like Clarkesworld readers to know about you, your work, or *All That We See or Seem*?

Thanks for reading. I hope all of you reading this will meet Julia Z in *All That We See or Seem*. I'm wrapping up work on the second Julia Z book now, and it's even more fun. Can't wait to get that one out too.

Arley Sorg is an associate agent at kt literary. He is a two-time World Fantasy Award Finalist and a two-time Locus Award Finalist for his work as co-Editor-in-Chief at *Fantasy Magazine*. Arley is also a SFWA Solstice Award Recipient, a Space Cowboy Award Recipient, and a finalist for two Ignyte Awards. Arley is senior editor at *Locus*, associate editor at both *Lightspeed* & *Nightmare*, a columnist for *The Magazine of Fantasy and Science Fiction* and an interviewer for *Clarkesworld*.

Editor's Desk: Nineteen
NEIL CLARKE

October marks the nineteenth anniversary of our first issue. Each time this month comes around, I'm amazed by just how much time has passed. In previous anniversary editorials, I've written about our origins, obstacles we've faced, and the goals we have. Being able to pay our staff a more reasonable wage remains our top priority, but with our twentieth anniversary looming on the horizon, I think we also need to make room for celebration.

While I have some basic ideas, I'm not entirely sure what that should look like. Running a magazine makes sense to me at this point. Planning something to recognize a milestone like this? That's way outside my lane. By starting things now, though, I'm hoping that the process can be less stressful and more collaborative. I'm very interested in hearing what our community thinks we should do to mark the occasion. While budgetary concerns will be a factor, don't let money limit your thoughts at this brainstorming stage. No idea is too large or too small.

There are some things I do know. I can say that we won't be soliciting stories from past authors. While we'd love to see them return to our pages, their stories should still come through the open submissions process we have committed to. Abandoning our values for a special occasion wouldn't be true to what has made us who we are. New authors are just as much part of celebration as the old.

It's also important for us to recognize that our audience and authorship is global. While in-person events won't be shunned, we want to make sure that we offer opportunities to include those that can't get to us or we can't get to ourselves. Given the difficulties for international travelers to the US at the moment, I am looking at possibly going abroad for some events, like Eurocon. And yes, there should be virtual events as well. Optimally, we should partner with existing events or conventions, so if you are involved in something that could fit the bill, please reach out. We'd love to find a way to connect with as many events as possible.

In other words, we want to make our twentieth anniversary year something special: a year-long thank you to everyone that made it possible to reach this milestone. I can think of no better way to do this than to involve our incredible community in the planning process and hope you'll take the opportunity to toss in your two-cents. Feel free to reach out in whatever way you like, but email (neil@ clarkesworldmagazine.com) is probably best.

Thank you once again for your continued support.

ABOUT THE AUTHOR

Neil Clarke is the editor of *Clarkesworld Magazine, Forever Magazine,* and several anthologies, including the Best Science Fiction of the Year series. He is a four-time winner of the Hugo Award for Best Editor Short Form, two-time winner of the Locus Award for Best Editor, a four-time winner of the Chesley Award for Best Art Director, and a recipient of the Kate Wilhelm Solstice Award. He currently lives in NJ with his wife and two sons.

Overgrowth
COVER ART BY QUENTIN STIPP

Made in United States
Cleveland, OH
23 October 2025

24545859R00095